The Quirks

AND THE

QUIRKALICIOUS

BIRTHDAY

Books by Erin Soderberg

The Quirks

WELCOME TO NORMAL

CIRCUS QUIRKUS

QUIRKALICIOUS BIRTHDAY

The Quirks

AND THE

QUIRKALICIOUS BIRTHDAY

ERIN SODERBERG

ILLUSTRATED BY COLIN JACK

BLOOMSBURY

NEW YORK LONDON NEW DELHI SYDNEY

WARNING! This might *look* like a normal book, about normal people, in a normal place . . . But get ready to celebrate a most unusual birthday with THE QUIRKS!

First published in the United States of America in January 2015
by Bloomsbury Children's Books
www.bloomsbury.com

Bloomsbury is a registered trademark of Bloomsbury Publishing Plc

For information about permission to reproduce selections from this book, write to Permissions, Bloomsbury Children's Books, 1385 Broadway, New York, New York 10018

Bloomsbury books may be purchased for business or promotional use. For information on bulk purchases please contact Macmillan Corporate and Premium Sales Department at specialmarkets@macmillan.com

Library of Congress Cataloging-in-Publication Data
Soderberg, Erin.
The Quirks and the quirkalicious birthday / by Erin Soderberg ; illustrations by Colin Jack.
    pages   cm
Summary: Twins Molly and Penelope Quirk are excited about Grandpa Quill's annual birthday scavenger hunt, but as they seek mini gifts leading up to one special tenth birthday present, they argue about what kind of pet they hope they will receive until they are fighting nonstop.
ISBN 978-1-61963-370-4 (hardcover) • ISBN 978-1-61963-371-1 (e-book)
[1. Family life—Fiction. 2. Magic—Fiction. 3. Twins—Fiction. 4. Sisters—Fiction.
5. Treasure hunt (Game)—Fiction. 6. Gifts—Fiction. 7. Birthdays—Fiction.]
I. Jack, Colin, illustrator. II. Title.
PZ7.S68525Qm 2015
[Fic]—dc23
2014010207

Book design by John Candell
Typeset by Westchester Book Composition
Printed and bound in the U.S.A. by Thomson-Shore Inc., Dexter, Michigan
2 4 6 8 10 9 7 5 3 1

All papers used by Bloomsbury Publishing, Inc., are natural, recyclable products made from wood grown in well-managed forests. The manufacturing processes conform to the environmental regulations of the country of origin.

For all the teachers and librarians who help put the right books in kids' hands. Thank you for making me a reader.

Table of Contents

1: Stinky Siblings ——————————— 1

2: Quirkalicious Birthday Hunt ——— 3

3: Double Trouble ————————————— 14

4: A Surprise for Saturday —————— 27

5: Pesky Party Planning —————————— 34

6: *Poof!* Potbellied Piggies ———————— 45

7: Teatime Treasure Hunting ————— 56

8: Pierce Von Fluffenfluffer —————— 67

9: Stars of the Week ———————————— 73

10: Sugar Monster ——————————————— 84

11: Fetch, Finn! ——————————————— 91

12: Please Pass the Taco Bake —————— 102

13: Rhymes with "Horn" ————————— 114

14: Corn Niblets ——————————— 124

15: Attic Attistant ——————————— 133

16: Escape! —————————————————— 141

17: Follow the Blume —————————— 150

18: Nerdy Cow ——————————— 162

19: Follow the Sounds —————————— 172

20: What's Dat? ———————————————— 181

21: A Quirky Party ——————————— 193

CHAPTER 1

Stinky Siblings

Sometimes, siblings stink.

There are times when they literally stink: after accidentally stepping in dog poo, or going on a bath strike, or eating too many chives fresh from the garden. But sometimes, they stink in the *other* way. Little brothers, twin sisters, siblings of any kind . . . anyone with a sister or brother knows that other kids in your family can really get on your nerves now and again.

Most of the time, the kids in the Quirk family got along very well. Sure, Finnegan Quirk pestered and picked on his sisters an awful lot. Molly bossed and got frustrated too often. And Penelope caused lots of interesting problems with her magical mind. But they all loved and supported one another—no matter what.

In fact, Molly and Penelope Quirk were not just twin sisters; they were also best friends. But every so often, even twins—*especially* twins—have trouble getting along. There are times when twins can't or just don't *want* to cooperate, days or weeks or months when it's impossible to agree about nearly everything.

That is the position the Quirk girls found themselves in during the week leading up to their tenth birthday. Turning ten is a big deal, double digits and all that. But for two girls in Normal, Michigan, turning ten was also about to become a very big mess.

CHAPTER 2

Quirkalicious Birthday Hunt

"Molly, wake up!" Penelope Quirk balanced on the edge of her bed and shook the rail of her twin sister's top bunk. She poked Molly's pillow and whispered directly into her ear. "Wakeupwakeupwakeup! It's time!"

Molly rolled over and groaned, wishing for just a few more minutes of sleep. She wrapped her pillow around her head like a giant stuffed taco and squeezed her eyes closed. She felt so sleepy. "Ergh," Molly muttered groggily. Then she sat up quickly, and her pillow-wrapped head bonked against the

3

ceiling above her. She was suddenly very much awake. "Is it Monday?"

"Yep. The best week of the year officially starts *now*." Penelope pulled off her pajamas and threw on her T-shirt. She drummed her hands on Molly's bed again. "Da da da da! Birthday week! And our Quirkalicious Birthday Hunt! Ten ta ten ten *ten*!"

Molly scrambled off her bunk and grabbed the shirt and jeans she'd laid out in a neat stack the night before. No one in the Quirk family was very organized, but both Molly and Penelope had recently started laying out clothes each night for the next morning. Penelope found it made her feel more in control of her day. Molly just liked having a few extra minutes to sleep. As Molly pulled her wild, brown curly hair away from her face with a headband, she asked, "Do you think Gramps remembered?"

Penelope jumped into her skirt and tugged it past her knobby knees. Two hops and one quick twist and she was dressed. "Oh, he remembered," she assured Molly. Penelope—who was often called Pen for short—pulled her crinkly curls back into a messy ponytail. She grinned at her sister's reflection in the mirror that hung over her dresser. "Ready?"

Molly nodded. "Set."

"Go!" Both girls hustled out of their bedroom and stampeded down the stairs. Early-autumn mornings in Michigan were often quite cold, so a chill nipped at the girls' fingers and noses as they ran through the house. But warm air floated toward them from the kitchen, making the house feel and smell like *home.*

Molly didn't realize how hungry she was until the smell of apple sausages and fresh currant scones hot from the oven made her stomach growl. "Yummers!" Molly ran to the stove, where their grandpa Quilliam Quirk was pushing little sausages around in a pan coated with melted butter. "My favorite breakfast!"

"Mine, too," Penelope agreed, plucking a piece off one of the scones. She stuck her finger into a little bowl of jam and dabbed it on the warm scone. She stuffed the gooey bite into her mouth, then reached out to pick off another bite.

Grandpa Quill playfully swatted her hand away. "Only the best for my birthday-week girls. I'll have

these tasty treats ready in just a moment. Your mom had the early shift at Crazy Ed's this morning, but she wanted me to pass one of these along to both of you." He held his arms out and wiggled them, waiting for a hug. But Molly and Penelope had already made their way to the table, where they were clearing a space for breakfast. The speckled kitchen table was a dumping spot for everyone's stuff, and each of the Quirks had gotten used to pushing random things aside to make room for meals each day.

The girls moved three pairs of Grandpa's reading glasses, a dirty Crazy Ed's mug, two empty soup cans, and one apron to make room for containers filled with clotted cream, jam, and marmalade for the scones. Grandpa Quill cleared his throat, still waiting for his hugs. "Girls?" he prompted. When neither Molly nor Pen picked up on his hints, Grandpa Quill muttered, "Well, maybe we need to try that again."

Suddenly, time swooshed and whipped backward, just like someone had pressed a giant REWIND button. Moments later, Penelope and Molly rushed through the dining room a second time. You see, like most of the Quirks, Grandpa had a special kind of magic power—a "Quirk." Grandpa Quill's magic allowed him to have a do-over whenever he wanted one. He could rewind time, sending people spiraling backward a few seconds or minutes or however much time he needed to replay a real-life scene a second or third or fourth time over.

Molly was the only person, other than Grandpa Quill of course, who ever noticed time flipping and flopping. Molly always knew, because she was immune to the rest of her family's magic. She had no Quirk of her own, but at least she had immunity. Sometimes, being the only Quirk without a special magic power could come in handy—but sometimes, it really stunk being the only non-magical member of a very unusual family!

The girls came flying into the kitchen again. This time, Grandpa was in front of the scones, waiting with open arms. As he squished them both into a tight hug, Molly peeked over his shoulder. "Yummers!" she said again, giving her grandpa a wink. "Sausages and scones. My favorite."

"Mine, too," Penelope said, reaching for the scones.

Grandpa popped two toasty scones off the pan and tossed one to each of them. "Only the best for my birthday girls," he said. "Now have a seat and let's eat." He leaned into the dining room and yelled to Molly and Penelope's younger brother. "Finn! Breakfast's on!"

Penelope held the scone in her mouth as she and Molly shoved the clutter that was gathered on the table to the side again. Molly carried the dishes of cream and jam to the table, while Penelope tried to talk through a mouthful of scone. "Toe wuff nub fost pwewent, Wamps?"

"Pardon?" Grandpa Quill asked, stabbing a sausage with his fork.

Penelope swallowed loudly. "So where's our first present, Gramps?"

Grandpa Quill chuckled and squeezed into an empty seat at the table. He slowly pulled open a scone and covered it with cream and Michigan cherry jam. His long, droopy mustache was quickly tipped with the sticky red stuff. "Patience, dear girl."

"Patience?" Molly demanded. "We've been waiting a whole year for this Quirkalicious Birthday Hunt. Let's get moving, Gramps."

Five-year-old Finnegan Quirk echoed, "Yeah, Gramps, let's get moving!" as he bounced into the kitchen on an inflatable hopping ball. Molly watched her brother's messy tuft of blond hair spring up and down as he hopped back and forth across the linoleum floor.

Though Molly could see every one of Finn's bouncy-ball moves, the only thing Grandpa Quill and Penelope could see was the hopping ball, springing up and down without a rider. Because Finn Quirk also had a special kind of magic power. He was invisible, and the only person

on earth who could see him was Molly . . . unless he was chewing a piece of gum.

Finn had recently discovered that when his mouth was full of chewing gum, he was visible for the whole world to see. But because his jaw got tired from chewing gum all day at kindergarten, Finn often spent his hours at home gumless and invisible—partly because his mouth needed a break, but mostly because it was easier for him to make mischief when he was see-through. "Gramps, just tell us where you hid the first present. Point at it quietly or something. I can follow your finger to find it." Finn flashed his toothless smile, but it had no effect since Grandpa Quill couldn't see him.

Grandpa shook his head. "No, sirree, Mr. Finn. This Quirkalicious Birthday Hunt is just that: a scavenger hunt for the birthday girls. Molly and Penelope have to find their first present on their own, kiddo. No hints, or it's not as fun."

Finn pouted. When he remembered no one could see his lower lip jutting out, he popped a stick of gum out of his pocket and into his mouth. He immediately whizzed into view and pouted some more. "Please? Maybe just tell *me* where it's hidden? I'm a super secret-keeper."

"You know the drill," Grandpa said, resting his hands on his big belly. "The girls need to find their first present, which—like always—is hidden somewhere in the kitchen. They can start their search after breakfast. Inside the first present is a clue that will lead them to their next present and their next clue." He glanced at Molly and Penelope. "And so on. There are six gifts in total—five little guys, and then the big honker."

Penelope stared back. As if they needed a reminder about how the Quirkalicious Birthday Hunt worked! "We know, Gramps. We've been doing your birthday scavenger hunts since we were three. We're expert present hunters now, and besides, we make an excellent search team."

Grandpa Quill huffed. "I know you know how it works, but it's only fair to repeat the rules each time we do a Quirkalicious Birthday Hunt. I don't want anyone crying foul if things don't work out quite right. You kids have all been lucky that you've found every one of your presents in the past—but when you turn ten, you hit double digits.

That means this year the clues are going to be doubly hard." He leaned forward and his mustache dipped into his coffee cup. "As usual, you have until your actual, official birthday on Saturday to solve all the clues. The fifth and last clue will lead you to the big, final present. If you don't succeed, you can keep the little gifts you find along the way, but no super-duper mega-gift."

"But—" Molly blurted.

"No buts about it," Grandpa Quill interrupted. "If you don't solve all my clues, you don't get all your presents. And the scavenger hunt can't begin until you and Penelope find your first gift. We begin *after* breakfast. No exceptions."

Molly and Penelope looked at each other, then looked at the piles of delicious food on the table. Without another word, they each grabbed a scone and chowed down.

CHAPTER 3

Double Trouble

Double Trouble

"Look in the broom closet," Finn ordered. He was wiggling with excitement over the scavenger hunt. They'd all finished breakfast in record time and left the scraps on the table while Molly and Penelope searched for their first birthday present. Finn stood on one of the kitchen chairs and tried to direct their search. "Gramps hides everything in the broom closet."

Molly pulled open the door to the kitchen closet and several bits of broken bagpipe fell out onto the floor. She pushed them aside and dug through the cluttered mess that was hidden behind the door. "Shoes . . . a pair of Niblet's favorite socks . . . ew, Gramps, what is this?" Molly picked up something long and furry that sort of looked like a hairy scarf. She sniffed it, then threw it back on the floor and pushed it to the back of the closet with her toe. "There's nothing but junk in here."

Across the kitchen, Penelope had opened the flour and powdered sugar containers and was inspecting them for hidden gifts. "Nothing in here, either."

The girls got down on their hands and knees to check in all the corners and under the table. Then they searched in all the drawers. Finn helpfully climbed up onto the counter to check inside the Chimp-Chump clock on the wall. The swinging monkey tail bonked him on the nose as he peered inside. "Nubbin' here," he said, squeezing his nose.

Molly put her hands on her hips and gazed around the kitchen. Grandpa Quill sipped his coffee, rubbed his chubby belly, and smirked at her. "Where is it, Gramps? You usually make the first clue pretty easy to find."

"I told you—this year, your Quirkalicious

Birthday Hunt is going to be doubly hard. You're double digits now, ladies. Double the fun, double the work. You'll have to double up to find it."

"Enough with the double," Penelope grumbled. "Double this, double that, double . . ." Suddenly, second versions of Molly, Finn, and Grandpa Quill all materialized in the kitchen. The usually spacious kitchen was now very crowded with a whole lot of Quirks.

Molly's double stood beside her, chewing one of the leftover scones. Finn's double sat inside the silverware drawer and banged two forks together while singing "e-i-e-i-o." Grandpa Quill's double was sound asleep—snoring—with his head slumped against his chest at the table. Like the real Grandpa Quill, his mustache was tipped in jam.

Penelope's eyes grew wide. "Uh-oh." She squeezed her eyes closed and hummed, trying to get her overactive imagination to calm down. Both Molly and her double walked over to stand next to Penelope. Both Mollys rubbed Pen's hand, trying to be helpful. Pen's eyes snapped open again. "That's not helping, Molly, and, uh . . . other Molly." Her gaze shifted from one version of her sister to

16

the other, and back again. She shook her head and slammed her eyes closed. "It's creepy that there are two of you."

"Kinda, yeah," one of the Mollys agreed. "Any chance you can stop thinking about doubles?"

Penelope shrugged. "I'm trying." Penelope Quirk had an overactive imagination, just like most nine (and seven-eighths)-year-olds. But unlike all other nine- and ten-year-olds, Pen had a special kind of magic power. Sometimes, the secret thoughts inside Penelope's head came to life. When she was worried about something, or her mind was full to bursting with strange thoughts—*poof!*—the hidden bits of Penelope's imagination would become real. Just like that. Pen didn't have much control over her imagination, and her magic often caused a whole lot of problems. "Obviously I would never make a second Finn come to life on *purpose*. Two Finns are too much trouble."

Just as Finn joyfully joined his double to sing a round of "Row, Row, Row Your Boat," everyone's doubles faded away. Once again, there were only four Quirks in the kitchen. Four Quirks and a whole lot of magic.

"Okay then," Molly said, with no further comment. She was used to her family's magic. As the only non-magical Quirk, Molly found it was usually best to just pretend her family's Quirks were totally normal—in their own special way. The Quirks were unique and quite odd, sure, but Molly was beginning to realize the concept of *normal* was different depending upon whom you asked. Still, she did sometimes wish her family was a little better at fitting in with the rest of the world.

Molly glanced up at the clock. "Now that that's over, let's get back to the business of finding our first gift. We have to leave for school in exactly eight minutes."

"We can look for our first clue more after school, Molly. It's not like we have to find it right now." Penelope grabbed an orange out of the fridge to add to her lunch. She tossed an apple to Molly.

Molly frowned. "But we always find our first present before school on the Monday morning of our birthday week. *Always*."

19

Penelope grabbed another apple out of the fridge and took a bite out of it. She fixed her sister with a firm look. There were times when Molly was very bossy. "Well, sometimes things change."

"Not this," Molly insisted. "This is a tradition. Our *only* tradition. We're going to find the first present now, so we can search for the second clue after school."

Pen lifted her eyebrows. She tried to push back against her sister when she was being silly. But Molly could be very stubborn when she didn't get her way. "Oh, so you're in charge of our birthday scavenger hunt now, huh? You get to decide how we do everything?"

Molly's lips were set in a thin line. She said nothing, just sniffed and continued her present search.

"You'd better do what Bossy McBosserson says," Finn whispered to Penelope. Pen knew she ought not laugh, even though her sister really was being quite bossy.

Molly stuck her tongue out at Finn. Then she said, "What if it's a pet? We can't leave a puppy or a baby monkey or a potbellied pig stuck inside a wrapped box all day, right?"

Grandpa snorted into his coffee. "You think I

20

hid a monkey inside the first clue box? Or that I put a pig in the kitchen?"

"I hope you did," Molly said quietly. "You know we want a cute pet more than anything this year. We're almost ten. We can handle the responsibility."

Grandpa nodded. "I know you girls want another pet. You've mentioned it once or twenty times lately."

"It's just . . . ," Penelope started. She and Molly *did* want another pet, yes—but it wasn't just for them. "Niblet's been getting so lonely during the day. Now that Finn's going to school, and you never play with him—well, Nibbly gets bored."

When he heard his name, the Quirk family's pet monster peeked around the corner into the kitchen. His stuffed bunny was wrapped tightly in his hands. Penelope waved at him and blew him a kiss. Niblet hastily pulled his furry head back around the corner and hid in the shadows again. Only his super-teensy toes were still showing.

Niblet had gotten to be very good at hiding, since he knew that no one outside the family could ever see him. After all, a pet monster wasn't an entirely normal thing for an ordinary family to have. But all the Quirks agreed that sweet Niblet was one of the best inventions of Penelope's over-active imagination. One day she'd imagined a monster was hidden under her bed and—*poof!*—there he was. Unlike Penelope's other magical creations, Niblet had never disappeared. And that was a good thing, since every member of the family loved him to bits.

While the Quirk kids were off at school all day, Niblet spent most of his days snoozing under Penelope's bunk. But there were only so many hours in a day a furry monster could nap before he got a little bored. So he and the girls had decided another pet would be a great idea.

Now Niblet reached his hand out from the

shadows and waved a piece of paper in the air. He'd drawn a picture with a purple marker. Niblet wasn't much of an artist, but anyone could see that he'd drawn himself and some sort of other animal, playing fetch together. In the bottom corner of the page, there was another scribbled drawing of Niblet curled around something black and white and furry.

"See?" Pen said, pointing at the picture. "He's been begging for a friend. But even when I concentrate super-hard, I can't seem to make another critter appear." She grinned at Grandpa Quill and folded her hands into a begging pose. "With Normal working out as well as it is, it seems like this is the perfect time to get another fun pet, don't you think?"

The Quirk family had lived in Normal, Michigan, for just a few weeks, but they already felt more at home here than they had anywhere they'd lived before. Usually, the family moved after just a few weeks or months in a town, but they all hoped their time in Normal wouldn't ever come to an end.

"I think you should focus on finding that first clue so you're not late for school," Grandpa Quill replied. "And worry about pets later."

Penelope shrugged. "That's not a no to pets," she said to Molly. "A no is usually a solid no, but talking about it later means we're still at maybe."

Molly smiled. "Okay, so let's double up and solve this doubly hard clue."

Penelope hopped up on the counter. Her eyes grew wide as she had a thought. "Doubly hard . . . doubly high? Maybe we need to *literally* work together to find this clue."

Grandpa made a *ding-ding-ding* sound, like they'd won a prize in a game show.

Molly clapped. "That must be it."

"Do you want to sit on my shoulders so we can scope out some high spots?" Pen offered.

24

Molly stood on the counter, then climbed onto her sister's shoulders. They wobbled and wiggled, but Molly knew Penelope wouldn't drop her. As Pen weaved across the kitchen, Molly peeked into the uppermost cabinets. She found the top shelves were only filled with years-old dust from the last residents of their house. When Molly brushed her hand across the top of the clock, a ladybug that had been hiding there flew away. There were very few places left that they hadn't looked.

"Hey!" Penelope said, swerving toward the middle of the kitchen. "The fan's not on. Could he have hid it on one of the fan blades?"

Finn ran over to the switch on the wall and flipped the fan on. "I'll check."

The fan whirred around and around—but no present came flying off.

"Check the top of the fridge," Penelope suggested.

Molly peeked up onto the top of the fridge. It was stocked with boxes full of gum that their mom had ordered off the Internet. Fruity gum, gumballs, sugar-free sticks, and—"Doublemint!" She plucked the lone package of Doublemint gum out of an open box. Molly pulled out the last stick of gum. "It's just gum," she said, her hopes falling.

25

She got off Pen's shoulders, then looked inside the empty-looking package. On closer inspection, she realized a slim piece of gold paper was folded up and tucked inside. It was about half the length of a stick of gum. Molly reached in and pulled it out, then unfolded it. A little piece of gold—in the shape of an oval—fell out of the tiny piece of paper and clattered on the floor. Both girls looked down, confused.

"Is that our gift?" Penelope asked, looking a little disappointed. She picked up the golden oval and stared at it in her palm. "One weird piece of gold?"

Molly shrugged and studied the paper that had been wrapped around the gold, trying to decipher Grandpa Quill's scratchy handwriting. "I guess that's it. Whatever *it* is. Look, there's also a clue to help us find our second present."

> Among the blades you will find,
> Another gift you will not mind.
> You'll play with this one in the yard,
> I hope this clue isn't too hard.

26

"Have a good day at school, girls," Grandpa Quill said, winking at them. "See you later for more Quirkalicious hunting!"

CHAPTER 4

A Surprise for Saturday

When the Quirk kids arrived home from school that afternoon, their mom was waiting for them at the bus stop. "How was your morning?" Bree asked. "I hear you found your grandpa's first clue." She placed a kiss atop each girl's head, then knelt down to let Finn climb on her back. Even though Bree was often exhausted after spending the whole day on her feet at Crazy Ed's diner, where she worked as a waitress, she always had a little more energy and a lot more smiles when she saw her kids. Finn wrapped his sticky little

27

arms around her neck and burrowed his face into their mother's crazy hair as they began their walk home.

"We did," Penelope said, easily keeping pace with her mom as they walked along the narrow sidewalk. "Do you have any idea why he gave us a piece of gold?"

Bree shrugged. "I might have some idea."

"What's the deal?" Molly asked.

"I suspect everything will become clearer later in the week—all will make sense in good time," Bree replied with an amused smile. "For now, I need to take you girls shopping to get some supplies for your party—and we need to do some planning." She looked at each of her daughters in turn. "I assume you want a birthday party?"

Molly and Penelope both slowed, then stopped in front of their house. Neither girl said anything. The wispy branches of the willow tree in the Quirks' front yard blew in leafy tendrils around them as they stood still as stone. Their neighbor Mrs. DeVille poked her stubby nose out from between her closed living room curtains. She lifted her hand in a curt wave, then closed the curtains up tight again. The Quirks' neighbor wasn't exactly the friendliest lady in Normal, but they had gotten to know her a little better in the past couple of weeks and knew she wasn't all bad, either. Finn was certain she actually *liked* them, but Molly thought she merely *tolerated* the Quirks.

The twins looked at each other with wide eyes, then gaped at their mother. Finally, Molly said, "A birthday party? For us? For *real*?"

"Why not?" Bree asked. "You girls are making some nice friends here in Normal. Why not celebrate such an important birthday with a fun party?"

"Like, a party with friends and everything? Or a party with just the family?" Penelope gulped. A family party was one thing . . . A party with friends was another thing altogether.

"If we do something simple, you can have ten kids apiece. Invite one person for each year you've been alive."

"But," Penelope began. She choked on her words, then swallowed and started again. It felt like there were small pebbles jiggling around in her stomach. "But we've never had a friend party before. And I, uh, don't really know ten people."

"So invite one. Or two. However many you like." Bree's voice was carefree and casual, but they all knew this was a big deal. The Quirk kids had never lived anywhere long enough to make friends, so the idea of them actually having a birthday party that involved any kind of guest list was serious business. Finn popped off his mom's back and scurried up the front walk to toss his gum and get an afternoon snack.

Bree knelt down in front of Molly and Penelope and said, "You both know we've never had a big birthday party for you girls before because we've never really had a place to call home. But why not have your first-ever party in Normal? It's worth a shot, don't you think? This is our home now, and I think it's important that we do everything we can to make ourselves feel settled."

"Yeah," Molly agreed, leaping joyfully into the air. "Let's do it!"

30

Penelope muttered something under her breath. Her smile was weak. "Sure? Why not?"

Bree clapped her hands excitedly. "Then let's go on a little outing and talk about where to have your party. We could do something basic here at

the house . . . or we could make it a costume party . . . or go to a movie . . . or, what else do kids do for birthday parties?"

Molly smiled, her mind spinning with ideas. She and Pen had only ever been to one party before. It was at their new friend Stella Anderson's house, and it was a sleepover. She thought a sleepover was a little too much for their first party ever, so what else could they do for their birthday celebration?

Bree ticked off their to-do list on her fingers as she headed toward the Quirks' big van. "We need to get invitations, and we should probably load up with some snacks and plates and balloons, and get this party planned. We'll have it on your actual birthday—Saturday. You girls have a lot of planning to do before then." She beamed, obviously happy she'd been able to deliver such fun news.

Molly forgot all about finding their next Quirk-alicious Birthday Hunt clue, and hopped in the van to go to the party supply store.

As they buckled up, Penelope tried to imagine herself having a great time at her own birthday party—opening presents, hanging out with the few friends she'd met in Normal, playing games, and eating cake. Pen commanded her thoughts to stay positive, though her imagination was threatening to run wild with all the things that might go wrong on their big day. Despite the fact that she and Molly would be in the spotlight throughout most of the party—*gulp!*—it would all go just fine. At least, Pen really *hoped* it would. If things turned sour, their birthday party could become a good-bye party.

CHAPTER 5

Pesky Party Planning

Finn came along for the ride to Party Stop, sitting invisibly—but not quietly—in the backseat. There were just a few stores in the small town of Normal, so they had to drive to the next town over. Finn told knock-knock jokes from the moment his seat belt was buckled until the van was parked again, making it a long ride. Molly didn't even realize there *were* that many knock-knock jokes about cows and buffalo and toots.

Inside, the store was empty of people, but packed with *stuff*. All kinds of things, more than any of the Quirks could ever imagine anyone would need for a simple party. Streamers, balloons, and cake-decorating supplies were stacked three adults tall on shelves that towered over them like mini skyscrapers. Party invitations grinned at them, face out, from a long rack on the wall. Plates and cups and napkins were organized in rainbow order, from the front of the store to the back.

When she stood in the center of one of the aisles, Molly felt almost as claustrophobic as she had the time they'd visited New York City, despite the fact that there were no other shoppers in the store. She and Penelope both looked up and saw that the ceiling was dripping with piñatas—crepe paper animals and cupcakes and castles of all different colors and sizes.

"How about we get a cow piñata?" Molly immediately suggested. "That would be fun."

"Piñatas are cruel," Penelope countered instantly. "All those people swinging bats and sticks at some poor animal, trying to break it open so they can get candy? It's wrong."

Molly rolled her eyes. "Piñatas are a tradition. A party tradition."

"How do you even know that?" Pen snapped. "It's not like you've been to a thousand parties."

"I just do," Molly said, even though she didn't know. She'd seen lots of piñatas at parties on TV, and they seemed fun. "Why are you being so crabby about it anyway?"

"I'm not crabby," Pen growled. "I just don't want a piñata, okay?"

"Well, I do want a piñata." Molly crossed her arms. "I'll get one for *my* party." Usually, she and her sister agreed about almost everything. But Pen was being weird, and Molly didn't feel like dealing with her bummer attitude. Who on earth thought piñatas were *cruel*?

Penelope narrowed her eyes. "*Your* party? Isn't it *our* party?"

"We're both turning ten, aren't we?" Molly demanded. "We both get a party. Double the fun, as Gramps would say. It's just that our parties are happening at the same time, in the same place. If you're going to say no to everything I want for the party, then I'm going to plan my own thing, and you can plan *your* own thing."

"Mom's not going to let us have two separate

parties, and you know it. And besides, I'm not saying no to *everything*. The only thing I've said no to is the piñata," Penelope argued. "I think they're kinda dumb."

Molly turned and walked away, muttering, "Well, I think that's dumb."

Pen chased after her. "What did you say?"

"Nothing."

"Molly, why are you being mean?"

"I'm not being mean," Molly shouted. "I just want my first-ever party to be perfect. And I don't want people to come to the party expecting a piñata filled with candy, and then find out that there's no piñata and think my party is stupid. All because you think piñatas are *cruel*."

"Girls!" Bree whipped around the corner, her arms loaded up with bags of colored balloons and packages of candy. "What is this all about?"

"Nothing," Molly and Penelope said together.

"It certainly sounded like something." Bree looked from Molly to Penelope, waiting for one of them to explain. Neither girl had any intention of tattling on the other, but it was obvious that *something* was up. "You never fight. What is going on?" She gave them a serious look.

Molly knew their mom could convince Penelope to tell her anything, if she wanted to. Bree Quirk was blessed with the power of mind control—she could make people do or think whatever she wanted. *Most* people, anyway. Like Grandpa Quill's rewinding and Finn's invisibility, Bree's magic never worked on Molly, either. But Molly did most of the things her mom told her to do anyway, simply because she was her mother.

Bree tried not to use her magic on her family unless it was a really serious situation. She felt like her magic power was a little too much like trickery and lying, so she used her powers mostly when the Quirks were in a real scrape and needed to explain their way out of magical messes.

"Dun-dun-dunnnnnn . . . ," Finn said, sounding ominous. "Turning ten is a messy mess mess."

"It's nothing," Molly said to their mother again. As Bree and Finn walked away, Molly glanced at her sister and blurted, "Forget the piñata for now. Let's just keep shopping for other party stuff." She made her way down an aisle filled with themed plates, reaching out to touch some that she liked. "Look at these, Pen. Aren't they cute?" She held up a package decorated with a pug wearing glittery green sunglasses.

"Yeah, but I like these better," Penelope said, unwilling to let her sister boss her into all the decisions. She pointed to plates with a picture of a cat wearing a tiara. "You know I'm more of a cat person. They're so cute and cuddly. And funny."

"And I like dogs," Molly shot back. "They're more interesting, and friendlier, and they run around and chase balls and stuff."

Pen and Molly hadn't yet been able to agree about what kind of pet they wanted, if they were to get a new pet. And though they were simply looking at pictures of animals on party plates at that moment, Pen knew they were really back to the same old argument about what kind of pet each girl would prefer to have. She announced, "But dogs are all wild and wiggly. Cats are calmer and they purr."

Molly looked away from the plates and faced Penelope. "But dogs are sillier. And we could play fetch and take it on walks. They're so bouncy and

40

energetic and it seems like everyone except us has one."

Penelope could tell Molly was in a fighting mood, so she decided to change the subject. Arguing with her sister was the pits. Molly was more of a blurter who liked to argue about stuff right away and try to solve things immediately, while Penelope preferred to walk away from conflict and come back to talk about the problem later when everyone had calmed down.

Molly had always been really good at distracting Penelope when her magic was acting up—maybe, Penelope thought, she could distract Molly from her grumpy attitude in the same way so they wouldn't have to argue about cats versus dogs right there in the party store. "Hey, Mol, if we did get a pet for our big birthday present, do you think Gramps might buy us a capuchin monkey? Wouldn't that be cute?"

Molly unfolded her arms and smiled a tiny smile. "Are capuchins those little monkeys that get to wear diapers?"

Pen giggled. "I guess any monkey could wear a diaper. Do you think they're hard to potty train?"

"Probably." Molly laughed. "Maybe we should ask for an iguana or something that can pee in its own environment."

"Ooh!" Pen said, getting excited about all the different pets they could ask for. "What about a snake?"

Molly shivered. "Snakes kind of creep me out. I still like the idea of a potbellied pig. Can you imagine how cute it would be if we put our pig on a leash and walked him down the street?" She waddled down the aisle, acting like a toddling pig. Then she stopped suddenly, caught on a mental image of herself walking down the streets of Normal with a pig in tow. People would point and stare and think she was . . . well, crazy. And utterly strange. Suddenly, the idea of a silly pig didn't seem so perfect. The Quirks were strange enough *without* a pig on a leash.

Just then, a loud snort reverberated from the deepest part of the shelf behind them. Both girls jumped, then scrambled to push aside boxes of plastic forks to see what was hiding among the party supplies. An adorable little piglet peeked out at them from the shadows. Molly grabbed Pen's hand and pulled her down the aisle. "Maybe we should get your mind off pigs?"

The pig oinked as Molly and Penelope walked away. Penelope couldn't stop thinking about it back there . . . all pink and soft and alone. How long would it stay back there before it disappeared again? Would it behave, or did she need to worry about the pig falling off the shelf and running through the aisles?

"Maybe we should just keep asking for a normal pet, like a dog or cat?" Molly said, trying to distract her sister. "If we want to fit in, I'm not sure a barrelful of monkeys or a potbellied pig is going to help." She tried not to laugh, but found it impossible.

Penelope giggled, too. "A weird pet won't really let us slip in under the radar, will it? Unfortunately, neither will a diaper-wearing monkey."

"Nuh-uh." Molly shrugged.

Pen considered all the possible animals they could get for a pet, and how cute Niblet would be, surrounded by plump pigs and colorful iguanas and tiny monkeys and chattering parrots and . . .

Penelope's eyes suddenly went wide. "Uh-oh!"

CHAPTER 6

Poof! Potbellied Piggies

Before Pen could stop it from happening, the images in her mind began to come to life. Her thoughts swirled and whirled. All around them, the animals she'd been imagining became real in a burst of magic.

Poof! Oink!

Poof! Woof!

Poof! Chitter-chatter-cheep!

One by one, dozens of animals popped up out of thin air and within seconds, the girls were surrounded by critters. It was like they were in the middle of a zoo. Monkeys swung from the piñatas on the ceiling, pigs tumbled over one another, puppies of all colors and breeds chased each other through the aisles, and kittens knocked over boxes of arts and crafts. The party store had become a pet store in the blink of an eye.

"Hey!" The lone shopkeeper came running toward them just as Bree and Finn zipped around the corner with armloads of stuff. "You can't bring animals in here!" His gaze went from the pigs to the lizards to the puppies, and his eyes grew wide. "How did you—?" He trailed off.

"I—" Pen tried to explain, but as was always the case, there was just no logical explanation for the things that could happen when Quirks were around. "I take my pets everywhere?"

Molly groaned. Finn whooped with joy as he leaned down to tickle a bunch of puppies.

"How did you even get all these animals in here?" The shopkeeper—whose name tag said: I'M ERIC, AND I HELP MAKE PERFECT PARTIES!—looked utterly stumped. "I don't know what you kids are up to, but this is a—"

Bree interrupted. "Let me explain, Eric." She

dropped everything she'd been carrying and walked over to him.

Eric batted at a parrot that had landed on his shoulder. He yelped as it flew away, then looked at Bree, whose voice was calm and commanding. Molly knew her mother was about to use her magic. Eric would never even know what had really happened. He'd just sort of *forget*. Bree would convince him that the animals had never been there at all.

Molly watched closely as her mother fixed her gaze on Eric and smiled brightly. "I'd like to sug-gest that you take a quick break in the back of the store, Eric. Enjoy a nice cup of coffee, kick your feet up, relax. We'll have things back to normal in no time, and then you should just forget you ever saw any of this today. Deal?"

Eric shrugged and grinned. "Sounds like a good plan to me."

"Thanks for your understanding." Bree's smile wobbled. Whenever she had to use her magic to make people forget, she got a little faint and dizzy. If she tried to control more than one mind at a time, it was even worse.

Molly ran over to the candy aisle and grabbed her mom a chocolate bar. A bite of something sweet often helped restore her energy. Bree unwrapped the candy, popped a chunk into her mouth, and sighed.

The animals were still running loose. The chaos that surrounded them was keeping Penelope from focusing. Until she relaxed, her magical mind would continue to go wild.

"This isn't fair," Finn whined. "Do Molly and Pen get to keep all these animals? That's the best present ever."

"Of course we're not keeping the animals," Bree snapped.

"Can I just keep one little piggy?" Finn asked. "I like the one with spots. He matches the blankie on my bed."

Molly shushed him and turned to her sister. "Pen? You've got to concentrate. Stop thinking about dogs and monkeys and anything that snorts, okay? Let's just think about our party . . . and the Quirkalicious Birthday Hunt that's waiting for us at home . . . and maybe we can talk about what kind of cake we should get for the party?"

"Cake?" Pen said, squishing her eyes closed tight. "I love cake."

"I know you do," Molly said calmly. "So let's talk about that instead of pets, okay?" Out of the corner of her eye, Molly watched as Finn took his gum out of his mouth. She knew he was invisible to everyone but her now. Her eyes narrowed, keeping a close eye on him as he crept down the aisle toward the pile of plump piggies. Her mom and Penelope could no longer see him, and that made Molly nervous. But she'd just have to hope that her brother wasn't going to do anything too terrible while she worked on calming her sister's mind. "Should we get a chocolate cake, or vanilla?"

Penelope's eyes were still closed as Molly watched some of the animals begin to disappear. It almost looked like someone had taken a giant eraser and scrubbed the spot where the kittens had been wrestling just a moment before. Then the dogs disappeared in a flash. Then the monkeys, who were still swinging from piñata to piñata, began to blur before they were gone altogether. "I like vanilla cupcakes with raspberry filling. And swirly flowers on the top."

Molly cringed. She had really hoped they could agree on a big, fudgy chocolate cake, but she figured now wasn't the best time to argue. Even though she hated tiny cupcakes with swirly frosting flowers, she just said, "Okay. Tell me more about your dream birthday cake." Molly could tell her sister was relaxing, but the little pigs were still scrambling around at the far end of the aisle. Molly watched as Finn chased after them, reaching his arms out as though he was going to—

"Finn!" Molly yelled, pulling away from Pen. "Do not touch that pig."

Penelope's eyes shot open before the pigs had a chance to vanish like all the other animals had. Finn looked at Molly, then back at the potbellied pigs. He grinned, then dove for the little spotted pig he'd been eyeing earlier. The pig squealed as Finn caught it around its middle. It squirmed and snorted, trying to break free from Finn's invisible arms. But Finn held tight and bundled the itty-bitty runt up in his arms until it stopped squirming and sniffed to figure out who or what had him.

Bree gasped. The only thing she could see was a pig suddenly floating in midair. Quickly, Finn

wrapped the pig up inside the bottom of his invisible shirt to try to hide it from his mom. The parts of the pig that were covered by Finn's T-shirt were invisible, but the pig's head was still showing.

"Finnegan Quirk, you drop that pig right now." Bree put her hands on her hips. She wasn't using her magic—she was hoping a little mom-power would work.

"No." Finn stamped his foot.

"You need to let go of that pig so that your sister can focus."

"I want a piggy!" Finn screamed.

Bree was furious. "You cannot have a pig, and that is final." She moved toward the half-invisible pig, and held out her arms. "Think about Penelope, and the fact that we need to clear up this mess and get out of here already."

"It's not fair that Molly and Penelope get presents and a party," he said, sulking. "I want presents, too. I want a piggy. Just one little spotted piggy."

Bree spoke gently. "It is not your birthday. You will get presents when you turn six. And of course we'll have a party for you, too." Bree grabbed for the wriggling spotted pig, but Finn backed away. "Finn, as hard as it is to remember, you know this week is not about you. Molly and Penelope already share their birthday with each other—this week, you need to step aside and let them have the spotlight."

"Penelope *always* has the spotlight," Finn grumbled, sitting down on the floor, holding the pig tight.

Pen argued, "That's not true!" She narrowed her eyes at Finn, then looked to Molly for confirmation.

But Molly didn't say anything. Because the fact was, deep down, Molly kind of agreed with her brother. Penelope's Quirk required more time and effort than anyone else's did, and that often led to her getting more attention from their mom and Grandpa Quill. Plans often changed because of Pen; Molly always had to help her sister fit in at school before she could focus on making her own friends. Of course, the rest of the Quirk magic caused problems, too, but Molly was hyperaware of her sister's needs.

Molly knew that Penelope sometimes hated her magic, and because of that, she tried hard not to resent her for it. But sometimes, Molly thought, it was hard to be the twin who didn't need as much special attention. Sometimes, she wished they were all a little more equal. Sometimes, she wished she could just think about herself.

"Finn," Molly said finally. "You need to let the pig go. It came from Penelope's mind, and now that's where it needs to return. It wouldn't be fair to take it home with us."

"I'd take care of it!" Finn promised. "I would be better about taking baths if piggy could hang out in the tub with me. This little piggy went to bath time, this little piggy came home . . ." Finn tickled the pig's ears. "This little piggy loves roast beef . . ."

"Finn," Molly warned. She reached for her sister's hand again, and whispered to both Pen and Finn, "Just let it go."

Slowly, hesitantly, Finn released the pig from his invisible shirt and it trotted toward the check-out lane. As calm settled over the Quirk family once again, each and every one of the potbellied pigs vanished into thin air. Just before Eric returned from the back room, the last little piggy went *wee-wee-wee* and disappeared forever.

CHAPTER 7
Teatime Treasure Hunting

Afternoon tea had recently become a regular daily celebration at the Quirks' house. If you happened to be passing by and were lucky enough to get a peek inside the fenced-in backyard, it might have looked as though everything was highly ordinary and up to snuff—a few old folks gathering to chat and sip and snack.

The teapot was served on a checkered tile tray, with a small pot of honey and a dish of lemon wedges on the side. Cream was kept in a cow-shaped pitcher (and poured out of the cow's chipped ceramic nose, which was a bit gross). Cookies were presented on a rotating selection of holiday napkins that were decorated with fireworks and smiling ghosts and festive wreaths.

Most everything about teatime seemed normal— everything, that is, except the people who sat together for tea each afternoon. The Quirks' neighbor Mrs. DeVille was one member of the afternoon tea team. Grandpa Quill often joined, as well. The other was Gran Rose Quirk. In almost every way, Gran Quirk was an ordinary grandmother. Every way, that is, except for a few key things: she was approximately the size of a sugar-coated Easter Peep and was severely allergic to the indoors. So she lived outside in a small birdhouse-like home that the Quirks carried with them from town to town.

Mrs. DeVille and Gran Quirk had recently become unlikely friends. Every afternoon for the past week, they'd spent several hours together on the Quirks' back deck, enjoying each other's company while they watched Molly, Pen, and Finn play.

"Kid!" Mrs. DeVille shouted to Finn in the yard

as she dunked a chocolate shortbread cookie into her tea. "You're holding the baton wrong. Try it like this." Mrs. DeVille stood up and demonstrated the proper way to juggle a baton. Despite her creaky knee and wobbly arms, she made it look simple. Mrs. DeVille had a history with the circus, and she had been showing Finn how to improve his juggling technique. Mostly, she just muttered grumpy suggestions from her chair, but Finn did seem to be improving.

Molly and Penelope were relieved their brother was occupied, since it kept him out of their hair while they hunted for the next clue in their birthday scavenger hunt. They'd searched for a short while after they'd arrived home from the party supply store the night before, but their mom had forced them to come inside when it got dark. They'd spent the rest of the night analyzing their first clue to try to narrow down their search area:

Among the blades you will find,
Another gift you will not mind.
You'll play with this one in the yard,
I hope this clue isn't too hard.

Usually, Grandpa Quill didn't hide more than one present in the same room, so the kitchen was out. Since the clue said they'd play with this present in the yard, they figured that would be a good place to start their search. But so far, they'd come up empty-handed. The twins agreed that "blades" was probably referring to some sort of sharp gardening tool. So right after school, they'd gotten back to searching in both the front yard and the backyard and in the small, cluttered garage that was squeezed between the alley and the back fence.

"Girls, would either of you like a spot of tea?" Gran asked, fluttering toward Molly and Penelope. "Barbara and I are enjoying some made with dried mint leaves from my garden."

"No thanks, Gran," Molly said. "Pen and I really need to find our next clue. Gramps has never made the Quirkalicious Birthday Hunt so hard before."

"I'm starting to think he was going easy on us on purpose all these years, and he's just been waiting for us to turn ten so he can torture us," Penelope added. "This next clue is super-hidden."

"I'm sure you'll find it," Gran said, returning to her seat beside Mrs. DeVille.

Molly sat in the grass and tried to think. "Blades. Hidden among the blades." She leaned back and closed her eyes. She could hear Mrs. DeVille yelling at Finn to relax and take his time with his juggling. He looked like a water bug, the way he was zigging and zagging all over the yard, tossing his batons up at random. "What are we missing?"

"Well, there are shoulder blades," Penelope said. "And knife blades. Shovels have blades, right?" They'd already checked in and among the tools and had no luck. "Skate blades!" Pen said suddenly.

Molly sat up straight. "Yes! Let's check the sports stuff in the garage. I think it's all still packed in boxes from the move." She jumped up and ran toward the garage.

Penelope edged past an old lawn mower and pushed aside a stack of boxes filled with old clothes. "Here it is!" She pulled a box open and began to pull out a random collection of stuff.

"Any skates?" Molly peeked over her shoulder.

"No. Oh, wait." Penelope tossed some tiny pink winter boots aside and tugged something out of

the bottom of the box. "Skates!" She peered inside them and shrugged. "No gift."

"Ugh." Molly plunked down on the floor and leaned up against a stack of old phone books. "I'm starting to think there's a chance we might not find all our clues this year."

"We'll be fine," Penelope said. "We have until Saturday to find the rest of Gramps's clues."

"Saturday," Molly repeated. "I can't believe we're actually having a party on Saturday." She glanced at her sister. "Are you nervous?"

"A little," Pen admitted.

"Don't be. It's going to be great. Have you had any ideas about where we should have it? What about the water park in Durban? Do you think that's too expensive?"

"Probably," Pen said. "What about going to the movies? I asked Mom about that, and she said it would be okay."

"Maybe." Molly shrugged. She peeked at Penelope out of the corner of her eye, then said, "I was talking to Stella about our party at school today, and she thinks we should definitely have a piñata, no matter where we have the party."

Penelope chewed her lower lip. She muttered, "If Stella likes piñatas so much, why didn't she have a piñata at her own birthday party?"

"I don't know," Molly said. "But I told Mom I definitely want a piñata, and I think I want a chocolate cake. A big one. Cupcakes are never enough."

Pen opened her mouth to protest, but Molly charged on. "I was thinking, maybe we could have separate cakes. I know you want vanilla cupcakes. But I really want chocolate."

"I do want vanilla," Pen said quietly. After a long pause, she asked, "Do we need to make gift bags?"

"Probably," Molly said. "What if we had a tie-dying party, and then everyone could take their tie-dyed shirt home at the end as their present? That would be fun, right?"

Pen shrugged. Molly was full of ideas, but Pen had spent most of her time the past twenty-four hours focusing on how she was going to keep a lid on her magic at their party. "I guess tie-dyeing is okay."

"Or, what if we went to the park, and maybe we could have a water gun fight?" Molly asked, trying to get her sister excited. "Or water balloons?"

"Actually, I think I really want a movie party," Pen said, finally. The idea had popped into her head, and she figured she ought to say something—or Molly would just charge forward without her. "We never go to the movies. We could all get popcorn, and maybe everyone could come dressed like a movie star . . ."

"That sounds so boring," Molly blurted.

"Not to me," Pen argued. "I like movies. And it's too cold for water balloon fights anyway."

"Listen, grumpy, you're acting like a wet noodle about this party," Molly said abruptly. She tried to keep her voice kind, since she knew her words would sting. "I know you're worried about the party. But I'm really excited that we finally get to have a real birthday celebration, and I think you should be, too. We can't just watch a movie in a dark room with no one talking. That's super-boring. You can't always be nervous about your magic acting up, or you're never going to enjoy anything."

"I know," Pen said, rolling her eyes. She and Molly had had this conversation many times before. Penelope was working on her confidence, but it wasn't always easy for her to relax in new situations. She sometimes wished she could just sit in a corner and watch everyone moving around her, like the whole world was on TV.

While Molly longed to blend into the world around them, Penelope often felt safer when she was on the outside of everything. When Pen was too mixed up in the middle of things, she feared her magic might make her do something that would make people laugh at her—or think she was strange. "It will be great. It's just . . ." Pen paused. "It's hard for me to get excited about the party since you and I keep arguing about what kind of party we want. I hate fighting with you, and it's bumming me out."

"We're not fighting," Molly argued. "We're discussing." She glanced at her sister again, and realized Penelope did look glum. Pen was pretty sensitive, so Molly knew she should probably say she was sorry. But she really wasn't sorry. It wasn't just *her* fault that they were disagreeing about everything—Pen kept rejecting all of her ideas! "I just want the party to be perfect."

"Your idea of the perfect party is different from my version of the perfect party, though." Pen slid down to sit next to her sister and wrapped her arms around her knees. "Right?"

"I guess," Molly said with a shrug. "Maybe we should just keep looking for the next clue. Hopefully Gramps hid a better present this time. But we're never going to find it if we just sit here all day."

"Yeah," Pen agreed. "Should we split up, so we can look in more places?"

Molly nodded. For the first time in her life, the idea of splitting up from her twin sister actually sounded pretty good.

CHAPTER 8

Pierce Von Fuffenfluffer

The next morning, both Quirk girls woke up feeling utterly miserable. Though they'd split up and searched for their second clue everywhere the night before, they hadn't found it. So Wednesday morning they both sat silently at the breakfast table, picking at their toast without talking at all. Then they shuffled to the bus stop and rode to school in silence.

Even though it was neither girl's fault that they hadn't yet found their second clue, they were each irritated with the other. Their party planning feuds were creating friction, because both girls were overcome with worry. Would it be fun? Would Penelope's magic somehow ruin it? Could Finn behave? What if they didn't know enough about birthday parties to plan the perfect, normal party for their friends? They'd only been to one party ever before—it wasn't like they could just *copy* Stella Anderson's party.

"Guys!" Stella ran over to Molly and Penelope as soon as they climbed off the bus. "I can definitely come to your birthday party this weekend. I told my mom you were going to be giving me an invitation later this week and my mom said it's fine. I already picked your present. My mom said I could either choose one little present for each of you, or a big present for you guys to share. I decided it's better if I get something you can share, since bigger presents are way better and you guys share almost everything all the time anyway."

Finn, who'd been trailing behind the girls as they walked through the playground toward the front door of Normal Elementary School, tapped Molly on the shoulder. "Pierce can come, too."

Molly spun around. "Pierce who?"

Finn crinkled his nose. "Pierce from table four."

"Who is Pierce from table four?"

"Pierce Von Fuffenfluffer. He's in my class." Finn giggled.

"Pierce Von Fuffenfluffer?" Penelope asked, laughing along with their brother.

"That's not actually his whole name, but I never remember the last part so I call him Fuffenfluffer, like my favorite sandwich. It's something like that. I think. Also, I talked to Henry, Ruby, and Sam K., and they all said they just have to ask their moms. Well, Sam K. said he'd talk to his dad." Finn scratched his head. "He told me his dad is in charge on the weekends because his mom deserves a break."

Molly held up her hand. "Finn, your friends aren't coming to the party."

Stella giggled. She didn't have any younger brothers or sisters, so she got a big kick out of Finn whenever he hung around them on the playground.

"Why not?" Finn asked. "I'll be bored if I don't know anyone."

"You'll know us," Pen said. "And you've got Gramps."

"Gramps will just spend the whole party tickling me. I'm inviting friends."

"You can't!" Molly announced. "It's my party, and I don't want a bunch of kindergartners running around."

Pen cleared her throat. "*Our* party."

"Exactly," Molly said. "Pen and I are turning ten. Not you."

"Well, hoodley-toodley-too." Finn blew a raspberry. "Someone's just mad that I found the second clue in their Quirkalicious Birthday Hunt."

Molly and Penelope looked at each other, then back at their brother. "What?" they said together. "You did?"

"Uh-huh," Finn said. "I found it yesterday night. But I'm not going to tell you where it is unless you let me invite Pierce Von Fluffernutter to the party. And the other kids from table four." He paused for a second, then added, "Also table five."

"I thought it was Fuffenfluffer," Stella interrupted.

"Foofenpoofer," Finn said. "Or Fuddlepuddle.

Whatever. He usually just goes by Pierce." Finn did a little dance and sang out, "I found your second clue! I found your second clue!" Then he ran toward the kindergarten classroom and left Molly, Penelope, and Stella standing by the twisty slide.

"What if he did?" Pen said to Molly. "What if our five-year-old brother found our second clue before we did?"

"It doesn't matter," Molly said certainly as she and Pen walked with Stella toward room six.

"The fact that he claims to know where it is gives us a bigger clue. The only place he was yesterday afternoon was the backyard. So it must be hidden somewhere in the yard. Probably over by the deck, where he was juggling."

Penelope's mouth made a little O. "Blades of *grass*," she said. "It's hidden 'among the blades' *of grass*!"

Molly smiled brightly. Pen was an excellent clue-solver. "That's gotta be it. Woo-hoo! We'll find it this afternoon, for sure. You, sister, are awesome." She draped her arm across Pen's shoulder, then Stella linked arms with Molly on the other side and they all skipped into their classroom together.

CHAPTER 9

Stars of the Week

"Heidy-ho, ladies." Normal Elementary School's fourth-grade teacher, Mr. Intihar, was standing just inside the door to room six. For the third day in a row, he was wearing his special birthday tie. Mr. I. had a rainbow bow tie he wore all week when they were celebrating someone's birthday. Their teacher had all kinds of birthday traditions. When it was someone's birthday week, they got a ton of special privileges.

On Monday, the birthday kid got to decide what game the whole class would play during choice time in gym. On Tuesday, Mr. Intihar got everyone—including all the teachers—to sing "Happy Birthday" super-loud in the cafeteria. On Wednesday, you got to bring in a special Star of the Week poster—with cool information about your life—to share with the whole class. On Thursday, Mr. Intihar let the class skip math to have a classroom party with extra recess. On Friday, the birthday kid got to be Student Teacher for a Day (performing important jobs like being the line leader and running the morning meeting and other fun business).

Molly had been looking forward to each new day of birthday week, but Penelope, who didn't really enjoy extra attention *or* extra recess, had been trying to ignore it all. She'd let Molly pick the game in gym on Monday, and she'd secretly listened to their mom's iPod when everyone sang to them in the lunchroom the day before. But today it would be harder to hide.

"It's a lovely morning for some Stars of the Week to shine, don't you think?" Mr. Intihar held out his hands for a pair of high fives. "Ms. Quirks: Are you ready to present yourselves to the class today?"

Molly nodded. Penelope groaned.

The girls had spent the weekend putting together their special "About Me" posters. A lot of the Quirks' photo albums were still packed from their move to Normal, but Bree had helped them dig out a few pictures so they could decorate their posters with cute baby photos and stuff.

Mr. Intihar grabbed the girls' posters from behind his desk and unrolled them. "Why don't we share your posters first thing, so we don't run out of time later this afternoon. We have math testing this week, and it always seems to get in the way of the good stuff. Blah, blah, blah, testing." He grinned. "Don't tell the people in charge I said that."

"I can go first, Mr. I.," Molly offered. Though they hadn't talked about it much, Molly knew Penelope had been dreading her presentation. She realized that Penelope might not want to present alone, since the stress of it could send her thoughts spiraling. "Or maybe Penelope and I could present together?" She glanced at her sister to see if they were on the same page.

Pen smiled at her gratefully. "Yes, let's do it that way."

"Are you sure? If you don't want to share the spotlight, we could also have one of you present your poster today, and one of you could present tomorrow instead? You've had to share a lot of your birthday week privileges, and it might be nice if you each got a chance to shine alone," Mr. Intihar said, looking from one Quirk girl to the other.

Penelope's eyes grew wide, and she shook her head.

Mr. Intihar shrugged and looked to Molly. "If you don't mind sharing the spotlight, be my guests."

If she were being totally honest, Molly would have admitted that she did *not* want to share the spotlight with her sister. They already shared almost everything—birthday presents, a bedroom, friends, and clothes, among other things. She wanted a chance to let her classmates see her as her own person, not as one-half of the Quirk twins. But she loved Pen, and she knew that sharing the spotlight was a better thing to do. Really, her sister was an important part of who she was, so presenting their posters together did make sense.

But Penelope must have sensed her twin's

hesitation. She leaned in toward Molly and asked, "Are you sure you don't mind doing it together?"

"Of course I don't mind," Molly said in a quiet voice while the rest of the class settled down and found their seats. "Eventually you're going to have to do some of this stuff by yourself, you know . . . but I don't want anything to happen that might force us to cancel our party on Saturday. I think we have to do whatever we can to make sure nothing goes wrong before then."

"Yeah, I totally agree." Pen nodded.

Mr. Intihar clapped his hands to call for attention. "Good morning, fourth graders. As you know, this week our Birthday Stars of the Week are Ms. Penelope Quirk and Ms. Molly Quirk. Since they're still relatively new to our fine town, I think we'll all find their Star of the Week posters interesting and informative." He galloped to the back of the classroom, then pointed to Molly and Penelope. "Ladies, when you're ready, take it away."

Molly waved to the class. "Hello, everyone. Uh, I—we, um—" She stammered over her words, suddenly nervous. Penelope swallowed loudly beside her, which didn't help.

The Quirks had spent most of their lives trying to fade into the background and make themselves less noticeable. For years, they'd worked hard to keep people at a distance so no one would find out more than they absolutely had to know about the family's magical oddities. They just wanted to be normal—and they were sure the only way they could seem normal was to share as little about themselves as possible.

"Uh, so . . . ," Molly continued. Penelope stared at her feet, holding her poster loosely by her side. "So we were born almost ten years ago, in, um, Ohio. But we didn't live there very long. Here's a picture of me and Pen when we were little." She stuck a piece of tape on the top of her poster and affixed it to the smart board. Molly pointed to the biggest picture—one of her and Penelope as toddlers, sitting on Grandpa Quill's lap. Grandpa Quill's mustache was long and droopy, just like now—but back then it was still brown, the exact same shade as Molly's and Penelope's wild curls.

"That's our grandpa Quill," Penelope chimed in, her words bubbling out of her quickly and suddenly. It took every ounce of her courage to speak up, but as soon as her mouth was open the words just seemed to spill out. "His name is sort of perfect, because his mustache is like an old-fashioned quill pen. When he's eating, it always droops into his food, then it drips all over the table. He could use his mustache to write with if he wanted to."

Everyone in class laughed. Pen beamed. Molly shot her sister a look—it wasn't like her to make fun of someone in the family, just for a laugh.

Molly continued quickly. She tried to sound confident, so that Penelope wouldn't feel the need to fill her silences. "We also have a little brother, Finn. He's five, and in Mrs. Risdall's kindergarten class."

"That's him," Penelope blurted, pointing to a picture of Finn that their mom had taken at Normal Night—their town's annual celebration—a few weeks earlier. Until recently, there were almost no photos of Finn, since he'd spent most of his life invisible to everyone but Molly. There were a bunch of pictures of Finn as a baby, in the months before he began to fade, but then there were none. Penelope yammered on. "Finn is what my mom calls 'a character.' He also likes to wander around the house in only his underwear."

Everyone laughed again. Molly was humiliated on Finn's behalf, but Penelope grinned widely.

"Our mom is a waitress at Crazy Ed's, out on Old County Road Six," Molly said, pointing to a picture of their mom wearing an apron with dancing chickens on it. "She's really great. We have the best mom in the world. She's funny, and she gives great hugs, and—"

Penelope cut in, "Mr. Intihar thinks she's pretty great, too." The whole class whooped and giggled and turned to look at their teacher.

Nolan Paulson whistled and yelled, "Woo-woo, Mr. I.!"

"It just slipped out," Pen whispered to Molly, who was staring at her sister with an open mouth. "But that's the truth, isn't it?"

In the few short weeks the Quirks had lived in Normal, their mom had gotten to be friends with Mr. Intihar outside of school. The Quirks had had their teacher over for dinner, Finn had started to become friends with Mr. Intihar's son, Charlie, and their mom even called the girls' teacher *George.* It was really weird to think about teachers having first names, but Mr. Intihar asked them to Call-Me-George when he spent time with Bree.

Molly and Pen hadn't mentioned their mom's budding friendship with their zany teacher to any of their new friends in Normal. Based on Mr. Intihar's embarrassed expression and blotchy cheeks, he was obviously a little uncomfortable that it had come up now.

"Miss Quirk," he cautioned with an even voice. Mr. Intihar was rarely stern, but at that moment he looked quite serious. "I'd ask that you keep your presentation on the topic of yourselves and your family, and kindly leave me out of today's report."

"Sorry," Pen mumbled, blushing.

Molly felt sick. She couldn't believe her usually

shy sister was suddenly cracking jokes about their family in front of their whole class. In some ways, Molly would almost prefer that Pen's magic act up, rather than her mouth. *Magic* she could handle; this new show-offy comedian she could not. Pen's nerves were making her act unfamiliar and obnoxious.

"Anyway," Molly said, continuing to present the information on her poster in a straightforward manner. She pointed at pictures, shared simple facts about their family, and stole glances at her sister.

Throughout the rest of their presentation, Penelope managed to remain silent.

At one point, Molly noticed her sister had closed her eyes and gone totally still. Molly knew Pen's mind was acting up and her magic was threatening to cause problems. She was relieved that Penelope was able to keep her imagination under control. Because at that moment, standing up in front of her class beside her beloved twin sister, she wasn't actually sure she felt like helping her sister out of a bind. Molly had always been there to step in to try to help Pen take control of her Quirk. But now Molly was an itty bit curious to see what might happen if Penelope had to help herself.

CHAPTER 10

Sugar Monster

"I found it!" Penelope grabbed a small, square green package out from deep inside a patch of long, overgrown grass that was snaking out from under the deck. As soon as the bus had dropped them off on the corner that afternoon, Molly and Penelope ran home. They were eager to see if Pen was right about their clue being hidden "among the blades" of grass. Molly was still frustrated with her sister for the things she'd said during their presentation that morning, but she was hoping that some Quirkalicious clue hunting would help her forget about it.

"He wrapped it in green paper. It matches the grass perfectly. I can't believe Finn could see this," Pen said, holding the gift out to her sister. Molly grabbed it and turned it over in her hands.

"Should I open it?" Molly asked. Then she paused and said, "Wait. You open this one, since I got to open the first present."

"Okay, thanks." Pen snatched the present out of her sister's hands and tore it open. Under the wrapping paper, there was a plain cardboard box. Pen popped open the box and reached her hand inside. "A tennis ball?" Her disappointment was obvious.

"A tennis ball," Molly agreed. "Is that all that's in there?"

"Looks like there's a clue, too, but no other presents." Pen shrugged. "I guess Gramps expects us to share it." She looked up at Molly with a weird, crumbly sort of expression.

Molly's stomach twisted. She knew Pen felt just as bummed as she did. Their grandpa had hidden

a single tennis ball that they were supposed to use for . . . *what*? Neither of the Quirk twins played tennis, but maybe they were supposed to learn? "I guess we only need one ball if we're playing together, right? We would probably make a pretty good doubles team."

Pen nodded. "Do you think our big gift will be tennis rackets?"

"Beats me," Molly grouched. She and Pen had been sure Grandpa Quill and their mom had known how much they wanted a pet for their important tenth birthday. They'd been hopeful that their wish would come true . . . until the scavenger hunt mini presents were these weird, random things that made it seem like their grandpa Quill was maybe going a little crazy instead. "I really wanted a dog. Or a cat."

Pen squeezed her lips together, then said, "And I wanted a cat. Or a dog."

"Well, it's obvious neither of us is getting what we want," Molly blurted out, annoyed. "Clearly, Gramps has other ideas for this year's Quirkalicious Birthday Hunt."

In the past, the small gifts they'd found hidden around the house throughout their birthday week had been more fun. The treasures were things like new backyard games, or books they'd been eager to read, or a pair of glow-in-the-dark spinning tops. Usually, all the gifts were part of the same theme that all led up to a similar but much bigger gift. None of the Quirk kids had ever gotten something as random and boring as a single tennis ball before—their grandpa Quill tended to be much more creative and clever. And in the past, Molly and Penelope had loved sharing everything and working together during their birthday week.

So far this year, the girls could only agree on one thing: turning ten was also turning out to be the pits.

"What does the clue say?" Molly asked. "Let's get to work looking for it. We still have three more mini gifts to find before Saturday."

Penelope squinted to read their grandpa Quill's tiny handwriting.

> Under the fishy,
> Soft and squishy,
> Hidden among the posh.
> There you'll find,
> A gift you won't mind,
> When it's time to nosh.

"What's 'nosh'?" Molly asked.

Pen shrugged. "Beats me. Doesn't *posh* mean something fancy? We don't have anything fancy at our house."

Molly ran up the stairs that led onto the back deck. Gran and Gramps were setting up their afternoon tea service. Molly grabbed a cookie and asked, "Gran, what's 'nosh' mean?"

"Ah," Gran said, fluttering close to the girls. "If I told you, that would be cheating, now, wouldn't it?"

Grandpa Quill laughed and popped a cookie into his mouth. "Found your second clue finally, eh?"

"Yes," Molly said quietly. She didn't want to sound ungrateful, so she added, "We got the tennis ball. Thanks, Gramps."

"You're very welcome," he said, smirking. He obviously recognized the girls' disappointment. He tilted his head, saying, "It will all become clear in good time."

"That's what Mom said, too," Molly said, chewing her cookie as she followed Pen into the house. "Let's look up 'nosh' in the dictionary and see if it gives us any clues."

They ran upstairs. But when they pushed open the door to their bedroom, all thoughts of finding the dictionary vanished. There, in the center of their rug, was Niblet—spinning around and around in dizzy circles. Magic Markers and rough drawings of dogs and cats and pigs and monkeys were scattered all over the floor, and their monster was wobbling to and fro around them.

The usually sleepy and relaxed guy was also surrounded by empty packages of taffy, lollipops, fruit chews, and chocolates. His hands were filled with sweets, and his fur was sticky and rainbow colored where the candy had dropped and begun to melt into his warm skin. Niblet slowed his spinning and fell to the floor. His eyes went wide, he burped, and then their monster began to giggle.

CHAPTER 11

Fetch, Finn!

"Niblet!" Penelope exclaimed. "What's going on in here?"

Niblet looked from the candy stuck to his fur, to the piles of wrappers on the floor, to the empty space on the top of the dresser.

Molly groaned. "You ate the candy Mom bought for our party? That's supposed to be for Saturday!"

Niblet burped again, giggled, and rolled around the floor with a sad moan. He rubbed his tummy and tried to look sorry, but the sugar filled his scrawny arms and legs with uncontrollable energy.

He kicked and flipped around on the rug, plowing through the piles of empty candy wrappers and his own artwork. He looked like a chubby, sticky tumbleweed.

"Did he eat everything?" Pen asked, horrified. "That's a lot of candy for one monster."

Molly pointed to the floor next to Pen's dresser. "He missed some of the chocolate and the licorice."

"Oh, Nibbly," Pen muttered. "You're going to feel terrible." She leaned down and pulled Niblet in close for a hug. He squirmed in her arms, still loopy from all the sugar.

"We need to hide the rest of this candy somewhere. He's going to throw up. Now we barely have anything to put into the piñata on Saturday," Molly said. "Maybe we could hide the rest of the party stuff in the garage or something. Somewhere he can't get to it?"

"Yeah," Pen agreed. "Mom's going to be mad."

"We should have thought about Niblet before we put all the candy in our room." Molly felt responsible, somehow. She should have known better. "I was worried about Finn stealing everything if we left it in the kitchen. I didn't even think about

Niblet. This guy does love candy." She gave Niblet an affectionate pat on his back. It was hard to stay mad at him.

Pen nodded. "This is why he needs another little pet to keep him company. When he's bored, he gets into trouble. Just like Finn."

In response, Niblet bounced up and down on Pen's bed. Bits of sticky candy popped off his body and went zinging all over the room.

Molly walked toward the door of their bedroom with the remaining bags of party candy and supplies in her arms. "Let's see if we can find a good hiding spot in the garage to keep this stuff."

Pen started after her, but before the girls could get to the stairs, the door to Finn's room squeaked open. Invisible Finn peeked out of his room and waved at Molly. "You're looking for a good hiding spot in the garage, huh?" He giggled. "You're not going to find your next clue there."

"We're not looking for our next clue," Molly said. Then her eyes narrowed suspiciously. "But how do *you* know we're not going to find it in the garage?"

Finn was practically bursting with the secret he'd been keeping all afternoon. "Because I have it!" he squealed. "I have the third clue. And the third present. I found it and I took it!"

"How could you have it?" Pen demanded. "We just found the second present. You haven't even heard the next clue that would lead you to the next hiding spot."

Finn laughed harder. "Don't even bother looking for it, sisters. I already found it in the living room. The present is kind of dumb, though."

Molly pushed the door to her brother's room open the rest of the way. She dumped the party stuff in the hall, then scanned Finn's desk, floor, and bed. "Where is it?"

"Not telling."

"You know you're not supposed to butt in on our scavenger hunt," Penelope said. "Gramps will not be happy with you."

"*I'm* not happy with you," Molly added.

"Let me invite some of my friends to your birthday party, and then we can talk."

"Pierce Von Flufferbutter cannot come to our party," Molly insisted.

"You're mean." Finn pouted. "It's not fair that I don't get presents, or a scavenger hunt, *or* a party this week. Not. Fair."

"It's not your birthday," Molly reminded him.

"And you're not invisible . . . ," Finn muttered.

"What?" Molly stared at him—hard. "What did you just say?"

"I *said*, 'You're not invisible.' And I am. Nah nah nah *nah*." He danced around. "No one can hide anything when I'm around."

That's when Molly realized what had happened.

"You followed Gramps when he was hiding our clues! That's how you found the second clue in the grass so fast. And that's how you got to the third clue before us. You knew where they were hidden!"

"Not saying."

"That's cheating," Pen scolded.

"Gramps never said not to follow him. And he *knows* I'm sneaky." Finn pumped his fist in the air. "I followed him when he was hiding the second clue *and* the third clue! It was awesome."

"Give us our next clue and the present, Finn." Molly fixed him with her sternest look. "We need it so we can find the fourth Quirkalicious birthday clue on our own, without you butting in, please."

"No."

Penelope stamped her foot. "Give it."

"I am not a dog," Finn retorted. "You can't order me to do anything."

Suddenly, Finn's invisible backside sprouted a small wagging tail. He got down on all fours, stuck his tongue out of his mouth, and began to pant. Molly watched with horror as her brother became more doglike by the moment. He hadn't turned into a full-fledged dog, but he sure was acting like

one. She turned to her sister. "Pen! He is *not* a dog. Stop thinking that he is."

"He's the one who suggested it," Pen said casually. Though she couldn't see Finn, she knew what was happening to their brother, thanks to her magical imagination. She clapped once, then ordered, "Fetch our third clue and the present that went with it, little buddy."

Finn leaped across his bedroom on all fours. He growled and shook his body, like he was chasing after a squirrel, then squirmed under his bed.

A moment later, he swatted a flat, square package out from under the bed with his hand. Then Finn emerged—dusty, with a piece of paper clutched between his teeth. He leaped over to Pen and Molly, nudging the gift along in front of him. He spit the clue out in Molly's hand, then sat back on his haunches and waited for someone to give him an encouraging pat.

"Good boy," Pen said, grinning. As soon as she said it, Finn stopped panting and sat back on his tailless tush like a regular kid.

"That wasn't nice," Finn said. "You shouldn't use your magic to trick me."

"Huh," Penelope said, scratching her head as she gazed in Finn's general direction. "It's not nice to use your magic to trick people? That's funny, since—"

"Following Gramps around isn't the same as you turning me into a dog to fetch the present I was hiding from you," Finn snapped. "You tricked me."

Molly cut them off. "Neither of you should be using your magic to trick people." She turned to Finn. "So the third clue was in the living room, huh?"

Finn shrugged, offering no further details.

Molly cringed. "Our living room is *not* posh. It's kinda yucky in there, actually. With all that unfolded laundry, and Gramps's socks everywhere, and those funny throw pillows all over the place."

Pen gasped. "That's it! Under the *fishy*, soft and squishy . . . Gramps was talking about that ugly fish throw pillow, I bet. The one we got when we were living in Maine. Was the third clue hiding in the couch, Finn?"

Finn nodded. "The box was buried in there, nice and deep. You never would have found it without me."

Molly and Pen shared a meaningful look. "Well, then, I guess we owe you a huge thanks for all your help," Molly said. She figured it couldn't hurt to keep Finn on their side. "Pen, are you ready to find out what this thing is that we 'won't mind when it's time to nosh'?" Molly peeled the rest of the wrapping paper off the gift Finn had already opened for them. Then she pulled something out of the box inside.

Pen frowned and muttered, "It's a bowl. A boring white bowl."

"A bowl," Molly said miserably. "One bowl. To share. Again."

"I think Gramps is losing it." Penelope cradled the bowl in her hands and examined it. It was maybe a little bigger than ordinary bowls. "The cereal bowls *are* always dirty," she pointed out. "Maybe Gramps thought this would make it easier for eating breakfast?" As she said this aloud, Pen realized their new bowl wouldn't even be that great for eating cereal, since the bottom wasn't curved as much as a normal bowl. It was just sort of flat-ish.

"Why just one?" Molly wondered.

"I guess we have to find the fourth clue, and hope this whole hunt starts to make more sense soon." Pen unfolded the third clue and read aloud.

You throw away the outside,
and cook the inside,
Then you eat the outside,
and throw away the inside.
What am I?
(You'll soon find pieces of me hiding in
many a nook, corner, and knob.
You're on the right track when you
find my _____.)

"Okay . . . ," Molly said, trying to think. She glanced at Finn.

He burped. "I didn't see him hide the fourth clue. I got hungry and went to the kitchen for a snack, then I lost him. I don't even know if he's hidden it yet."

"So we're on our own for this one," Pen said. "Good. I think it sounds like it'll be fun to solve. It's a riddle!"

Before they could start to work through the clue, though, Grandpa Quill yelled up the stairs. "Girls! Finn!"

"Yes?" Pen hollered back.

"Dinner at Crazy Ed's tonight," he said. "Your mom's shift is just about over. Time to hop in the van and head on over for Potpie Wednesday. I'm a starvin' Marvin!"

"Okay," Molly said to her brother and sister as she folded the clue and tucked it into her pocket. "I'll go hide the rest of the candy and our party stuff in the garage. We can work on figuring out the riddle at dinner tonight. Then we can start searching for whatever the next mini gift is!"

Please Pass the Taco Bake

CHAPTER 12 ←

"I hear we have a very special birthday party to plan." Martha Chalupsky pulled a chair up to the back corner booth inside Crazy Ed's. Martha owned the restaurant where Bree Quirk worked, and she treated the family of her employees like she would treat her own family: with kindness, open arms, and lots of good food. After a rough early start with the Quirks, Martha had come to love Molly, Penelope, and Finn. She also hosted them—and sometimes Mr. Intihar—for dinner one night a week at Crazy Ed's. "I told your mom I'd be happy to whip up some food and bake you girls a delicious cake for your big tenth birthday party this weekend. What do you say?"

Molly and Penelope nodded eagerly. Martha patted them both vigorously on the back and laughed hysterically—this was her noisy form of affection.

"That would be awesome," Molly said, coughing.

"But no kugel," Finn muttered. He made gagging sounds and slipped under the table.

"We appreciate this so much, Martha," Bree said, shooting Finn a firm look. She'd just finished up her shift, and her apron was balled up on the seat next to her. She'd dumped her tips in the center of the table—Finn always liked to sort and count the coins as extra practice for his money unit in school.

"It's my pleasure. Anything for the Ed's family. Have you decided where you're going to have your party?" Martha took out an order pad. "That will help me figure out what kind of food we might need."

The girls shared a glance. "Not yet," Pen said. "We were talking about maybe going to the movies . . ."

"Or to the water park," Molly added quickly, stealing a peek at her mom. She caught her mom eyeing the small pile of tip money on the table, and realized a water park was probably too expensive. "Or we could just go to Grandview Park to have water-gun fights outside. That would be almost free."

"I think a lot of kids in town have their party at the roller skating rink," Martha said, just as Mr. Intihar strolled through the front door of Crazy Ed's. Mr. Intihar often just *happened* to drop by Crazy Ed's while the Quirks were having their weekly dinner. He usually sat at the coffee counter and ordered a slice of pie, then acted surprised when the Quirks invited him to join them in their booth.

Martha waved to Mr. Intihar and yelled, "Hey, George—didn't you have a birthday party at the roller rink back in the day?" Martha and Mr. Intihar had both grown up in Normal and never left. That's the kind of town it was.

Mr. Intihar waved back. "That I did. The big one-oh. When I turned ten. Can't believe that place is still in business." He grinned at the Quirks' table and added, "Top of the evening to you, Quirks."

Penelope saw her mom blush and touch her hair. The girls had noticed that Mr. Call-Me-George Intihar made their mom happy, so they liked when he came around. Molly and Pen knew as well as anyone how nice it was to find a friend in new towns. Pen scooted over and patted the seat beside her. "Join us, Mr. I.?"

Their teacher folded his long body into the booth and said, "Don't mind if I do. It's a real pleasure seeing your nice family here again. Sure makes my evening."

Martha picked up the birthday party conversation again while Mr. Intihar got settled. She tapped her chin with her pen and said, "The owner of the roller skating rink is a good friend of mine, so I could probably get you a great deal. It used to be a lot of fun, and they have a game room where you can have your snacks and open presents and stuff." She shrugged her shoulders and looked from Molly to Pen. "Just a suggestion."

Molly's eyes widened. "The roller rink is a great idea. What do you think, Pen?"

Pen chewed her lower lip and shrugged. She'd only ever seen roller rinks in movies. In movies,

there were often a lot of spotlights and the music was really loud and they seemed crowded and chaotic. Exactly the sort of place where her Quirk could go crazy. She thought it sounded awful. "I don't know. Roller skating?"

"Sounds fun," Molly announced. "It's decided then. Roller rink."

"Maybe we should talk about it a little more?" Pen suggested, frowning. "In private?"

"It's a great idea," Molly blurted out. "We can't talk about it forever, Pen." She was tired of trying to negotiate with Penelope about their party. Every time a good suggestion came up, Penelope shot it down. And also, she had to admit that she was still irritated about their Star of the Week presentation. Seeing Mr. Intihar sitting across the table, Molly remembered how uncomfortable she'd been about what Pen had said that morning. She felt like Penelope had betrayed them all, somehow. She'd broken their trust by making fun of the Quirks around others, and Molly was annoyed. Molly added, "We have to pick a place today, or we're not even going to get the invitations out before the party actually happens. It's in three days!"

"Everyone we're planning to invite already knows about the party," Pen pointed out. They'd told all their friends at school that their party would be on Saturday afternoon, and they had promised to hand out invitations soon. But since they were still figuring out (*fighting* about) the details, they hadn't gotten to them yet.

"The roller skating rink will be perfect," Molly said. She'd begun to wonder if Penelope was dragging her feet on purpose, in the hopes that they wouldn't have to *have* a party. That wasn't okay at *all*. "Mom, what do you think?"

"It could be a good idea." Bree gave Penelope a long look. "As long as you're both happy about it. Pen seems to have some concerns."

"We're both fine with it," Molly announced, before her sister had a chance to say anything more.

"What if we just did the party in our backyard?" Bree suggested. "We could hang decorations, and play some games. That would be the most affordable option."

Molly grimaced. "What about Gran?" she whispered to her mom. "And, um, Niblet?" She looked over at Martha and Mr. Intihar, who were both within earshot.

"We can figure that out," Bree said, seemingly unconcerned. "But I just don't think you girls are ever going to agree on a place you'll both be happy with. So our yard it is."

"A lot of kids in my class have their parties at home," Mr. Intihar said, obviously trying to help. "It is a good option!"

"You'll join us on Saturday, won't you, George?" Bree said, leaning across the table toward him. He nodded. "In our yard?" She looked at Molly and Penelope for final confirmation.

Even though a party in their backyard would be totally fine, Molly couldn't believe she and Pen had lost their chance to pick a more interesting spot because they couldn't agree on anything. It was their first party, and she wanted it to be spectacular! She sighed loudly and muttered, "The backyard will be great. Can we talk about food now?"

"Yes, let's talk about food," Gramps muttered. "Especially food that I can eat immediately, please."

As if on cue, their waitress sashayed over to their table. She had a huge tray loaded up with their dinner and a coffee for Mr. Intihar. Grandpa Quill rubbed his hands together and sniffed his potpie as soon as she'd set it down in front of him. "Delicious!"

Once they'd all begun to eat, the party planning continued. Martha began to suggest all kinds of foods they could have at their party—grilled cheese sandwiches, mini pizzas, a taco bake.

"Taco bake?" Finn screeched. His mouth was full of grilled cheese bits. "That sounds disgusting!"

"Finn," Bree scolded. "Martha is making suggestions. It's not your party, so you don't get a say in what food the girls choose to have."

"Taco bake sounds interesting," Molly said, trying not to smile. At least their mom was *trying* to let them figure out the party for themselves. "Let's have that."

"It's going to look like throw-up in a pan," Finn said, holding his small hand over his mouth while making retching sounds. "Think about it. Taco stuff, all smushed together, baked up with ooey-gooey cheese on top?"

"Finn." Bree nudged him to get his attention. "You don't need to eat it."

"I have to smell it," he said quietly. "And it's going to smell like—"

"That is enough!"

Molly peeked at Penelope, and realized that—as usual—her sister's imagination was acting up at the mere mention of gooey-looking food. Her face had a sickly yellow pallor, and her lips were white. Pen's eyes were squeezed closed, and she was humming quietly to try to get her mind off all the images that were *poof*ing into her head.

"Are you okay, Miss Penelope?" Mr. Intihar said, reaching out to touch her shoulder. Pen said nothing.

"Let's skip the taco bake," Molly grumbled. She did *not* want to worry that Pen's imagination might accidentally turn the food into throw-up at their party. Now that the suggestion was out there, there was no telling what might happen on Saturday. So Molly figured it was probably best to go with some safe food—once again, they had to plan around Penelope's Quirk. "Maybe we should just stick to the grilled cheese sandwiches or pizza or something."

"Grilled cheesy!" Finn cheered. "I pick that."

"Fine," Molly muttered. "Grilled cheese it is." Pen silently nodded in agreement, but Molly could tell her sister just wanted to get off the subject of food for the party. Mr. Intihar was still watching her closely. "What else would be easy for you to make, Martha?"

As they talked about side dishes and snack foods, Pen remained silent. Molly got to make all the decisions as Penelope struggled to keep her overactive imagination under control. Even when they began to talk about the cake, Pen just sat quietly—nodding her approval—as Molly told Martha all about the chocolate cake she'd been dreaming of. There was no mention of Penelope's vanilla cupcakes with swirly flowers at all.

After a few minutes of her sister's silence, Molly

realized something. When Pen was distracted and worried about her magic, she wasn't able to get involved in the party planning. That's when Molly began to wonder: Would she get to take over their party preparations completely if Pen's imagination just kept going wild? Perhaps, she reasoned, it would be a good idea for her to stop helping her sister rein in her magic for a few days. Would it be such a horrible thing if she just let her sister's Quirk go crazy?

Sure, Penelope would be miserable, and worried, and freaked out . . . but Molly wouldn't have to worry about negotiating everything about the party with her twin.

Before she could take the thought any further, Molly shook her head to clear it right out of her mind. *No*, she thought. *What kind of a sister am I if I don't help keep Penelope from being miserable? And what if her magic takes us right out of Normal?*

Overwhelmed by guilt for even thinking such a thought, Molly reached for her sister's hand under the table. She rubbed it until Penelope opened her eyes and began to smile again.

CHAPTER 13

Rhymes with "Horn"

"I've got it!" Pen exclaimed, sitting up in bed later that night.

"Huh?" Molly rolled from her back to her side and peered over the edge of her bunk. She'd just begun to fall asleep, and was having one of those fade-in-fade-out dreams about their dad. Molly and Pen still remembered a lot about him—the way he'd scratched their cheeks with his beard stubble on Sunday mornings, and the cinnamon rolls he sometimes made on special occasions. Sometimes they could even remember the sound of his quiet voice. He'd been shy and observant like Pen, and great at crossword puzzles and math like Molly.

Pen's face was illuminated by the moonlight streaming in from the side windows. Molly asked, "Got what?"

"It's corn." Penelope stood up on the edge of her bed and stared, wide-eyed, at her twin in the top bunk. "The answer to Gramps's riddle. You throw away the outside—the wrapper and the silky corn hair stuff—and you cook the corn. Then you eat the corn, and throw away the cob!"

Still half-asleep, Molly smiled groggily. "It is corn, isn't it? You are very smart."

"Yup." Pen reached her hand under Molly's blanket and fished around. "Lemme have the third clue. I need to read the rest of it, now that I figured out the riddle."

Molly giggled and stirred. "Hey, that tickles." She swatted her sister's hand out from under her blanket and grabbed at the piece of paper she'd hidden under her pillow. "Here's the clue."

"Okay. So next it says: 'You'll soon find pieces of me hiding in many a nook, corner, and knob.

You're on the right track when you find my blank.'
That's how it ends, with a blank."

"Cob," Molly murmured. "'Cob' rhymes with
'knob.' That's gotta be it."

Pen shrieked. "Yes! Cob."

"No shouting," Molly begged as Niblet stirred
under their bunk bed. "It's super-late."

Pen covered her mouth. "Sorry, no more yelling. But it is cob. We're right. What do you think it
means that we'll 'find pieces of me hiding in many
a nook, corner, and knob'? Oh!" She shrieked again,
then shushed herself. "I bet there are bits of corn
hidden around the house, but we're only close to
the clue when we find the cob. Yeah?"

"Yeah," Molly agreed. "Now can we sleep, and
we'll hunt for a random corncob first thing in the
morning?"

"Okay." Pen nodded. "Sleep tight, Molly. And
hey—" She blinked. "Thanks for helping me with
my magic and everything earlier at Crazy Ed's. I
don't know why I always have such a hard time
keeping control over my Quirk when we're at the
diner. There's something about Martha's food that
really gets to me."

Molly sighed. She still felt guilty for thinking about leaving Penelope to deal with her magic alone. But she was also still frustrated because of all the bickering about their party, and their Star of the Week presentation. "Yeah," Molly said finally. "No problem." She studied her sister's far-off expression in the light from the window, wondering what she was thinking. "Hey, Pen? Why did you say all that stuff about our family at school today?"

Pen shrugged. "I don't know."

"People were laughing at Gramps and Finn and Mom . . . and even at Mr. Intihar. Because of your words."

"I know," Pen whispered. After a long pause, she added, "I like the way it feels when people laugh at me because I'm funny. Usually, I'm just so worried about my magic and people staring at me like I'm crazy or something. Today, they were laughing because of something I *meant* to say, not because of something that happened by accident."

"I didn't like it," Molly said honestly.

"I could tell," Pen confessed. "But imagine how it feels for me. I'm standing up there, freaked out

that my magic is going to make me do something stupid, and then instead—*poof!*—I make everyone laugh in a good way instead. It was awesome."

Molly understood. She really did. She just didn't think she would have done the same thing Penelope had done in that situation. "Okay," she said finally. "But I'm still sort of mad at you."

"I'm sort of mad at you, too." Pen's lips were squeezed into a tight line. "You're being really bossy and selfish about our party."

"And you're being really stubborn and boring about it," Molly replied.

Pen took a deep breath in, then let a long breath out—she sounded like their mom when she needed a break, or after her magic had sapped her energy. Pen said quietly, "I've been wondering if maybe we should look for the rest of the clues in our Quirkalicious Birthday Hunt separately? Maybe if we weren't spending so much time together, we wouldn't fight so much."

Molly blinked back tears. She wasn't sad, exactly. Just kind of overwhelmed. "Yeah," she agreed. "With the scavenger hunt, and the party planning, and our birthday stuff at school . . . I guess maybe it is a lot of time together." *But we've always spent a lot of time together,* Molly thought. *And it's never been a problem before.*

"You've always been there for me, to help with my magic," Pen muttered. "But maybe I need to try to help myself a little more now."

Molly shifted uncomfortably in her bed. She was torn: one part of her wanted her sister to need her, to rely on her—after all, that's what sisters are for. But the other side of Molly had, just hours ago, wished Penelope would let her go a little bit, too. "Yeah, I guess. If that's what you want."

"I was also thinking about what you said about the party—that we could each just plan a few things we want separately, and that way we both get what we want." Pen twisted nervously at a curl behind her ear. "Should we stop trying to agree about everything, and each plan our own thing?"

Molly lay back on her pillow and stared up at the ceiling. "I guess we could do that. Then I can have my piñata."

"And you won't get in the way of my fancy cupcakes," Pen said, giggling. "We can talk to Mom and see if she'll let us each do our own thing—it might be more fun that way, anyway. Then we'll be a little bit surprised by each other's party plans. I'll do my stuff in one-half of the yard, and you'll be in charge of the other. You can have the deck, if you want."

"But we'd still have our parties at the same time, right?" Molly asked.

"Of course," Pen said. "We'll just get to plan different parts of it. I know you have all kinds of ideas for what you want to do at the party, and I have some other ideas . . ." She rested her chin on the rail of Molly's bunk. "The thing is, I feel like we have to figure out some way to stop arguing about everything. Maybe I'm wrong, but I can't help wondering: If we had been able to agree about the kind of pet we want, do you think Gramps and Mom would have taken our birthday wish more seriously? We keep fighting about whether we want a cat or a dog—"

"Or a monkey," Molly said, cutting her off.

"Or a monkey." Pen laughed. "We've been bickering about it ever since we first brought up the idea of a pet. Maybe that's why Gramps is giving us these weird mini gifts. We can't agree on anything, so he doesn't know what to get us. And now we keep fighting about the party. What if Mom decides to cancel it or something? Or what if she plans the whole thing without letting us get involved at all?"

Molly curled onto her side and looked at Penelope through the bunk rails. "So, we would split up to hunt for the rest of the clues in our Quirkalicious Birthday Hunt, and also do the rest of our party planning separately?" She felt a little bit sick to her stomach. Even though she'd been wishing she could distance herself from Penelope all week, the thought of actually getting what she wished for made her glum.

"I know that's what you want to do," Pen said, without any hesitation. "And we're just getting more and more mad at each other, which kind of makes birthday week stink. So, yeah."

"Okay," Molly said.

Neither girl said anything more. After a few moments, Pen retreated to her lower bunk and crawled under her covers. Molly could hear Pen's breathing—long and slow, but not asleep. And Pen could hear Molly tossing restlessly.

After a very long silence, Penelope said, "So I'll start looking for the corn in the morning."

"And I'll look after school," Molly said.

There was a long pause. "Good luck with your clue hunting, Molly."

"You, too."

It was nearly an hour before either girl was asleep. They each lay in their own beds, both wondering when they'd begun to slip so far apart.

CHAPTER 14

Corn Niblets

"How is the birthday hunt going?" Bree asked. She was sitting across the kitchen table from Molly on Thursday morning. The two of them were enjoying some rare one-on-one time. Penelope had gotten up early to eat a quick breakfast so she could start her search for the cob of corn before school. Gramps had just gone off on some sort of errand, and Finn had begged to tag along. "Are you and Penelope enjoying yourselves this year?"

"Yeah," Molly said through a mouthful of cereal.

She'd decided to eat her breakfast out of their new white bowl. Gramps had walked into the kitchen briefly while she was pouring Rice Krispies, and he'd laughed when he'd seen her using the new bowl—*laughed*! Like they weren't supposed to use it for cereal or something. "It's fine."

"Fine?" Bree frowned. She sipped her tea and leaned in toward Molly. "Usually you love your birthday scavenger hunts."

"It's good," Molly said gloomily. "The clues have just been harder than usual this year."

Bree smiled. "Ah. Taking too long to get to the big, final present, huh? Impatience getting the best of you?"

"I guess." She didn't want her mom involved in her fight with Penelope. Their mom would just worry, and she already had enough things on her mind without adding twin trouble. Molly pushed her bowl away and looked up at her mom. "Did you see the latest mini gift?"

Bree tilted her head toward the table. "The bowl? I did."

"I think Gramps might be losing it."

Molly's mom laughed. "He's always been kooky. But this? This bowl makes sense. It will make sense to you, too—soon enough."

Molly rolled her eyes. "You both keep saying that about all of the mini gifts. But I don't understand what a piece of gold, a tennis ball, and a random white bowl can possibly have in common. There's usually a theme with our birthday hunt. This year, it's just a bunch of weird stuff that Pen and I are supposed to share."

Bree didn't answer immediately. After a beat, she asked, "Don't you like to share?"

"Some things, sure," Molly grumbled. "But not everything."

"I see." Bree reached out to touch Molly's hand. "Is that what your gloomy mood is all about? Are you and Penelope having a difficult time planning your party and sharing your presents?"

"No," Molly said, staring down at the speckled table in front of her. She hadn't even convinced herself she was telling the truth, so she knew she hadn't fooled her mom. "Kinda."

"You don't need to agree about everything, you know. Just because you're twins doesn't mean

you have to like all the same things or do everything exactly the same way."

"I know."

Bree reached out to lift Molly's chin. "I know
you know. But sometimes, I think you choose to
forget that, because you're a good sister and you're
trying to make things easier for Penelope."

"Maybe," Molly said, wondering how her mom
had figured that out.

"I've known you for just a few days shy of ten years, dear heart. I know you care about your sister more than anything or anyone else in the world. But I also know that you are two very different girls, and sometimes it can be hard to compromise all the time." She smiled at Molly. "But I appreciate that you're trying to work things out between you. You make a good team."

Molly swallowed thickly, afraid to look her mother in the eye. Before Molly could confess that she and Penelope had decided to split up and work as two separate teams, rather than a partnership, Pen zoomed into the kitchen.

"I found some corn!" she cried.

"Where?" Molly asked.

"First, I found a tiny pile of kernels on the front porch. There were just a few little pieces kinda scattered on the corner of the railing. I think he hid more out there. Gran was keeping an eye on them, and she said she saw a squirrel munching away this morning. Then I found a smiley face made out of corn kernels in the corner of the dining room." Pen plopped into a chair and added, "But there was no cob either place. Just little bits of corn."

Molly took their new bowl to the sink and washed it—since there was only one, she wanted it to be clean if Penelope wanted to use it for her after-school cereal snack that afternoon.

"Also, I had an epiphany!" Pen said, leaning against the counter.

"What kind of epiphany?" Molly wondered. She liked the word "epiphany"—it sounded so cheerful and amazing. Like the good kind of magic.

"As I was searching for the corncob, I remembered that little bits of corn are called niblets," Pen said. "Corn niblets. Remember? That's what the packages in the freezer section at Food Mart say on the outside."

Molly closed her eyes and groaned. "I completely forgot about that. Do you think that means anything?"

"Maybe . . . ," Pen said. "Maybe Gramps wanted to include Niblet in the Quirkalicious Birthday Hunt somehow? Or maybe Nibbly's supposed to be an extra hint for this clue?" She closed her eyes. "Or maybe I'm just overthinking it."

Molly shrugged. "Did you look anywhere other than the front porch and the dining room?"

"I checked the porch, the living room, and I searched Finn's room—since he's not home." Pen glanced at their mom. "Don't tell him I was poking around in there, okay?"

"My lips are sealed," Bree said. "Anything goes when you're on a scavenger hunt."

Penelope grabbed both her and Molly's lunch bags out of the fridge. Molly tossed her sister one of the sandwiches she'd made before breakfast and said, "I can look in more places this afternoon. I was going to peek in the attic, and check the deck."

Bree glanced up at the clock on the wall. "You girls need to get going or you'll be late for the bus." She half stood, then returned to her seat. "Would you like me to walk with you to the bus stop today? Your grandfather is going to drop Finn off at school after his errand, so it's just the two of you today. If you'd like to head over there on your own, it's fine with me."

"Okay—thanks, Mom! We can walk ourselves." Molly grabbed her backpack from beside the door. Their mom was understandably overprotective. With a family full of surprises, a lot of things could go wrong. Bree tried to shield her kids from trouble when she could. But recently, she'd begun to give Molly and Penelope a bit more freedom. A perk, of sorts, for her almost-ten-year-olds. "See you later."

"Yeah, see you later, Mom!" Penelope added.

As the girls walked toward the bus stop, they continued to talk about the next clue. "I can help you look this afternoon," Penelope offered.

"No, it's okay," Molly said. "I said I'd search this afternoon, since you looked this morning. But if you want to hunt, too, go for it."

Pen nodded. "I think I will. We'll split up."

"Fine with me."

"Good."

"Well, good luck finding the next clue," Molly said as they approached the bus stop.

"You, too, Mol." Pen's throat felt tight as she watched for the school bus to come around the corner. She tried to think of the corncob, and the clue that would be wrapped beside it, and the big present that awaited them at the end of their scavenger hunt. "Only two mini presents left until our super present."

"Yep," Molly agreed. She considered the next two clues, and what it would feel like to find one or both of them without her sister by her side. Sure, she'd be proud of herself for proving she could do it alone. But it also wouldn't be the same.

As the bus pulled up, Molly and Penelope shared a quick smile. Even though they were supposed to be spending less time together, they still sat side by side on the bus. Some things just aren't meant to change.

CHAPTER 15

Attic Attistant

"I want to be your attistant." Finn trailed behind Molly as she ran up the stairs after school later that day. "Attistant Finn."

"I don't really need an assistant, Finn," Molly said. "Or an attistant. I like hunting for clues alone."

"That isn't true," Finn insisted with a resolute shake of his head. "You are a terrible treasure hunter."

"I am not!"

"You are," Finn said. "Penelope's way better at

this sort of thing. And if you guys are splitting up to search for the next clue, you need an attistant."

Molly stopped on the landing halfway up the stairs. Finn was right. She hadn't really thought about it before, but now that she considered it, she realized that this year—and in years past—Pen almost always found their mini gifts throughout the week. Penelope was the treasure-hunting pirate, and Molly was the . . . what? The pirate's parrot or something useless like that. She talked a lot, but did a whole lot of nothing.

On Monday, Pen had been the one to suggest they *double up* to find the first clue. Then, she'd been the one to realize that "blades" meant *blades of grass*. Next, Pen had figured out a way to get Finn to give up their third clue—by turning him into a dog. And just last night, she'd solved the corn riddle all by herself. Molly was useless. And now, working without her twin, it would be obvious just how useless she was. "Okay, Finn," she said finally. "You can be my assistant."

"Woo-woo-woo!" Finn cheered. "So we're looking for mini Nibblys?"

"What?" Molly continued to march up the stairs.

"Mini Niblets, right? I heard Pen say something about lots of Niblets."

"Corn niblets," Molly explained. "Gramps has us hunting for corn this time. There are little pieces of corn hidden all over the house, but we have to find the cob. That's where the next clue and mini present will be. At least, that's what Pen thinks."

"Where have you looked so far?" Finn asked, his eyes wide and serious.

"Nowhere," Molly confessed. "Pen searched a little bit this morning. She found some corn on the front porch and in the dining room, but no cob yet."

"So where should we start?" Finn asked.

Molly's eyes traveled to the rope that hung from the ceiling in the middle of the upstairs hallway where they were standing. If you pulled it, a little folding staircase lowered so you could get up into the attic.

"The attic?" Finn squeaked excitedly. "I love the attic!"

"Then you can go first," Molly said. "I'll climb up the stairs behind you, to make sure you don't fall." *And also so the bats will attack you first*, she thought guiltily.

Molly grabbed the stool from the bathroom and dragged it directly under the rope. She climbed on top and pulled. It took a few good tugs before the trapdoor began to budge. Then it fell from the ceiling and the folding stairs popped open. Finn cheered and stepped onto the first step.

When he reached the top, Finn gasped.

"What is it?" Molly asked.

"It's bee-yoo-tee-ful," Finn said. "Look at all this stuff!" Finn crawled across one of the beams that ran the long way through the attic. He pulled open boxes and *ooh*-ed and *aah*-ed about the stuff he found inside. "I'm gonna make a fort up here!"

While Finn nosedived into all the boxes, Molly searched for the corncob. The attic was stuffed with sealed-up cardboard boxes and itchy insulation. The only light came from two lone windows, one at each end of the room. Finn thought it was magical up here, but she found it kinda creepy.

Molly noticed that there were some recent footprints in the dust along the walkway. As though someone—Gramps?—had been up there sometime in the last few weeks. She followed the prints, but they led nowhere.

"I don't see anything," Molly said. "Did you find any cobs?"

Finn shook his head. "Nope, but I did find this." He held up a small, decorative box that was filled with tiny pieces of multicolored corn. There were purple pieces, and red, and orange, and yellow. It was like autumn in a box.

"Where did you find that?" Molly asked. She was even worse at searching than she'd thought. Thank goodness for Finn. Clearly, Gramps had hidden bits of corn absolutely everywhere.

"It was just sitting right over here," Finn said, pointing to an area where Molly had already searched.

Suddenly, Pen's voice carried up from the hallway. "Did you find something?" she asked. Molly could hear her climbing the stairs. "Sorry to interrupt your searching, but I just wanted to check in. See how you're doing . . ."

"We found more niblets," Molly said. "But no cob."

"I haven't found it yet, either," Pen said. She poked her head into the attic, joining them. "But I've found piles of niblets everywhere. In lots of nooks and corners, and even on the basement doorknob, like the clue said! Gramps obviously just likes hiding stuff—he's having fun. The niblets don't even *lead* anywhere. I think we can officially rule out the entire house."

"Where else have you looked?" Molly asked.

"Pretty much everywhere inside," Pen said. "The attic is the only place I haven't been, and you guys have that covered." Penelope was bored of searching by herself. She envied Molly—because at least she had Finn to hunt with. Penelope was lonely. The Quirkalicious Birthday Hunt wasn't nearly as fun without her sister as a partner. But she wasn't going to make it sound like she needed Molly. She didn't *need* Molly. Anyway, the girls had decided to work separately, and Penelope didn't want to give up already.

"I feel like Gramps has us on a wild-goose chase," Molly said. She was really frustrated.

"It's more like a wild-niblet chase," Finn said, giggling. Then he began to sing to the tune of "Itsy-Bitsy Spider." "Lots of little niblets, hiding around the housey, teeny-tiny goosies, chasing all around—" He carried on like this, singing and kicking his feet against the boxes in the attic.

"Itty-bitty niblets, hiding on the ground-let, super-cutie goosies, bopping up and down."

The song was catchy, and Molly felt herself start to bob her head along to his silly made-up tune. After a few moments, Penelope's eyes went wide. She backed down the ladder. "Oh, Finn," she said quietly. "You really shouldn't have . . ."

Squawk! Tumble!

Molly and Finn both hopped to their feet. In the hall below, their sister's mind had whipped up some serious chaos. Finn scampered down the skinny folding staircase for a closer look. Molly was right behind him.

Five itsy-bitsy geese and at least a dozen mini Niblets were running through the hallway.

"Uh-oh," Molly observed as one of the Niblets zoomed past her and did a clumsy somersault into the bathroom. Two other Niblets chased each other in circles in the center of Finn's bedroom, while a few others bounced on his bed. Several of the geese toddled toward the stairs and tumbled down them one at a time. "Now we're really on a wild-goose chase, aren't we?"

CHAPTER 16

Escape!

"Ugh," Pen groaned. She squeezed her eyes shut and tried to calm down. A moment later, the geese and bitty Niblets disappeared in a *pop!* "Sorry, guys."

"It's okay," Molly said, shrugging. "It happens." She made her way toward the girls' shared bedroom. "I'm surprised Niblet hasn't come out of our room to see what's going on. He loves excitement."

"That is weird," Pen agreed. "He must have slept right through it."

All three kids peeked around the door into Molly and Pen's room.

"He's not in here," Finn said.

Pen frowned. "Where could he be? He spends every afternoon napping under the bed. And it's not like him to wander off when we're all up here . . ." She focused on remaining calm, but was doing a terrible job of hiding her worry. Her forehead crinkled up and her mouth made a worried doughnut shape. She wondered if Niblet had been scared when he'd heard all the commotion in the hall and had run off somewhere without them noticing.

Molly rushed over to their comfy window seat. The window overlooking the side yard—and Mrs. DeVille's house—was open. There was usually a screen to keep out mosquitoes and flies, but the screen had been pushed up and fresh air blew through the open hole. The curtains rippled in the cool, gentle wind. "You don't think he . . . ?"

Penelope sucked in a breath. "Went out the window?"

"Uh-oh," Finn whispered. "He's in trouble. That is a no-no."

Molly kneeled on the cushions that padded the

ledge and peered down from their second-story window. There was a large wooden trellis that ran along the sidewall of the Quirks' house, with a flowering vine that climbed up and sprinkled lovely purple flowers across their plain white house. But after a summer of rain and sunshine, the vine had grown bigger than the trellis. At some point, it had spilled off the top of the wooden support and begun to slowly crawl up the sidewall. The vine's twisted arms stretched upward and leaves surrounded the outside of the girls' window like a picture frame.

Molly slumped down on the window seat and let her face fall in her hands. "I bet he's trying to find the rest of our birthday party candy," she said simply as everything clicked in her head. "He heard me say I was going to hide it in the garage. He must have gone after it. We were distracted by the scavenger hunt, and Gran and Gramps are busy getting their tea service ready, so he made a run for it when no one would see him."

143

"You think he jumped?" Penelope screeched.

Molly looked up and shook her head quickly. "No—I think he climbed down the vine."

"That is an excellent idea," Finn noted.

"It's very unsafe," Molly said, a warning note in her voice. She knew her brother *loved* ideas. "But it looks like he made it down just fine. He's not a splat in the side yard. Let's go find him."

All three kids hustled down the stairs and hightailed it to the back deck. Sure enough, Gran and Grandpa Quirk were busy bustling to and fro on the deck, getting everything ready for their afternoon tea with Mrs. DeVille. They wouldn't have noticed Pen's monster escaping even if he came over and pinched them on the bottom. Gran and Grandpa Quirk were in full prep mode, whistling and organizing and making everything just right for their special tea party.

Penelope led as the kids ran through the grass to the old garage in their backyard. Through the window, they could see that the garage was musty and dim. The service door was closed tight. Pen knocked her hip on the door to nudge it open.

"Nibbly?" she called tentatively. Niblet probably knew he was in big trouble—he was *not* allowed to leave the house without permission—so she had a feeling he was hiding behind boxes or old, stinky sports equipment. Molly took another small step forward. "You in here, big guy?"

No snuffs or grunts—just silence.

"Niblet?" Molly called, a little louder. She stepped past her sister and climbed up onto a chair. Then she reached—up, up, *up*—onto the top of the pile of boxes where she'd hidden the rest of their party stuff *way* out of reach. "Everything's still here."

"The candy?" Finn asked.

"Yeah. All of it. The piñata's still up here, and all the other bags of candy, too. Everything."

Penelope peeked around a pile of full-to-bursting bags of old clothes and peered inside the giant refrigerator box they always used to move Niblet from town to town. "He's not in his crate," she said. "But hey!" She dug down to the bottom of Niblet's box. "There's a trail of little corn niblets. They make a line across the bottom of the box. And look!" She crouched down and got closer. "An arrow! I think Gramps made an arrow out of niblets. In Niblet's crate!"

145

"What does the arrow point to?" Molly asked.

"Over here." Penelope squeezed around the

edge of the giant refrigerator box. "I found it!" From where they stood, Molly and Finn could only see the top of a dried ear of corn swinging in the air.

"Is there a present? A clue?" Molly wondered.

"There's a present!" Pen said. She squeezed back around the side of the box, and all three of them huddled around the brown-wrapped package. Pen handed the gift to Molly. "You can open it."

"Are you sure?" Molly asked, sliding her finger under the edge of the wrapping paper. When Pen nodded, Molly ripped off the paper and dug into the box. Her excitement faded when she saw what was inside. "A hairbrush. And stickers," she said.

"Stickers?" Finn asked. "Like, cool scratch and sniffy ones?"

"No," Molly said, pulling out the sheet of stickers. "Like, big, thick alphabet stickers."

"Oh," Pen said. "Is that it? One brush and some stickers?"

Molly shook her head. "There's also a clue. The clue is written in stickers."

"Well, that's kinda clever," Pen said, shrugging. "It's like a ransom note."

"What's a handsome note?" Finn asked.

147

Penelope giggled. "Ransom notes are the kind bad guys write when they want money from someone."

"Gramps calls me handsome sometimes. Does that mean I'm a bad guy?"

"Handsome and ransom are not the same thing," Molly said, also laughing. "Do you want to hear the clue?"

"Yes!" Pen said. "Read it."

Molly continued.

NOW THINGS WILL BEGIN TO
MAKE SENSE,
BUT FIRST YOU NEED TO CLIMB
THE FENCE.
GET OUT OF OUR HOUSE, OUR YARD,
OUR BLOCK,
AND FIND YOUR LAST CLUE WHERE
TEACHERS SQUAWK.
HINT: FOLLOW THE BLUMIE.

"School!" Penelope yelped. "He hid the last clue at school."

All three Quirk kids grabbed one another into a hug and danced around to celebrate. But their hug was cut short by a brisk knock on the open garage door.

Molly and Penelope whipped around and came face-to-face with Mrs. DeVille. The scowl on their neighbor's face made her look like a Halloween jack-o'-lantern. Mrs. DeVille cleared her throat and said, "Perhaps you kids ought to keep a closer eye on your belongings." Then she tugged at something just outside the garage door.

"Niblet!" Pen cried as their furry monster

stumbled around the corner into the garage. "Where was he?"

Niblet stared at the ground, his body shaking with worry.

"Your *dog*"—she winked at the Quirks. Molly smiled, sure this was Mrs. DeVille's way of promising to keep their secret—"seems to have gotten lost and found his way over to my side of the fence. Mind you, I'll let it slide this time. But don't let this *pet* wander onto my property again. I've got my hands full with . . ." Mrs. DeVille stopped speaking abruptly. Then she shook her head and blew out a long breath. "There's only so much I can overlook with you nuts. Only so much I'm willing to do. This guy nearly scared the living hee-haw out of me when he popped up on my deck, peeking in the window like he did."

As Mrs. DeVille hobbled through the yard, toward the back deck for tea, Molly called after her. "Thanks, Mrs. DeVille. We owe you!"

Mrs. DeVille grunted. "That's for sure." She turned back once, and Molly was almost sure she caught their grumpy neighbor smiling.

CHAPTER 17

Follow the Blume

When the Quirks arrived at school the next morning to search for their final clue, the halls were dim and quiet. Molly and Penelope had gotten up early, hurried through their breakfast, then pulled Grandpa Quill out the door to drive them so they'd have time to search before class started. Finn, who wasn't old enough to be left alone to get to the bus stop, came along for the ride.

"Let's split up," Molly suggested as they all stood inside the front doors near the office. "Penelope, you go that way, and I'll go this way." Molly pointed in the direction of the gym. She looked at Finn. Secretly, she hoped he knew where the last clue was hidden. "Finn, I guess you'll come with me again?"

Pen wasn't interested in arguing about it, so she agreed.

"Hold on a hoodly-hoo," Grandpa Quill said. He reached into his sweater pocket and plucked a bite off the piece of scone he'd brought along in a napkin. He popped the snack into his mouth, then washed it down with a sip of coffee from his travel mug. "Why aren't you girls hunting for your clue together?"

Molly and Penelope both shrugged. Finn spoke up. "They're fighting too much. So they decided to split up for the rest of their birthday hunt."

"Oh no-ho-ho." Grandpa Quill shook his head. "That's no fun at all."

"Neither is fighting," Pen muttered. Then she added, "It's fine, Gramps. Molly and I are better off splitting up to search. Really."

Grandpa popped another piece of scone into his mouth and grunted. "Well, whatever you decide. But it seems a shame to me. You girls are like chips and ketchup . . . better together. That's just my opinion."

The girls did split up. But both were quickly overwhelmed by the endless number of places there were to hide a gift at school. As they poked their heads into classrooms, bathrooms, and the gym, Molly and Pen both knew they had to narrow their search area somehow. If they didn't, they'd never find their last clue before the rest of the students arrived for class. And they only had one day left before their birthday. If they failed to find the last clue today, there would be no big, final present. And that would seriously stink.

Normal Elementary School was built in a circle—people could start to walk around one way, and eventually they'd be back to where they started. Just five minutes after each girl began their walk around the circle in opposite directions, they arrived back at their starting place—totally frustrated and overwhelmed.

Shoulders slumped, Pen said, "So."

Molly echoed, "So."

Gramps, who'd been following Penelope on her walk around the circle, settled onto one of the benches that lined the front hallway. "You girls need to use your noodles," he said. "Let's see some of that Quirk spunk."

"Can't you give us a little extra clue, Gramps?" Molly begged.

"Read the clue again," he suggested.

Pen pulled the clue out of her backpack and scanned it silently. "The main part of the clue leads us to school. Then there's the hint. 'Follow the blume,'" she said. "Are you sure you didn't mean 'bloom'? Like flowers? Did you misspell the clue?"

Pen and Molly sat on opposite ends of a bench. Each girl had her forehead in her hands, with bony

elbows resting on knobby knees. Finn plunked onto the bench between them, bouncing up and down.

"I meant what I wrote," Gramps said, taking another noisy sip of his coffee. He spoke slowly when he said, "Now think. Use what you *read* as your hint."

A moment later, Grandpa Quill rewound time. They'd flipped backward a few seconds, and once again he was saying, "Now think. Use what you *read* as your hint." He stressed the word "read" again, then added, "Use what you *read*: follow the *Blume*."

Molly—who was the only one who knew when Gramps was rewinding time—looked at him curiously to figure out why he'd gone backward and added to what he'd said. Grandpa Quill shrugged. Then he rewound once more. This time, he said pretty much what he'd said the first time. "Use what you *read* as your hint."

154

Molly shook her head and whispered, "No more rewinding," in a voice so low only Grandpa Quill could hear. She knew he was trying to help. But sometimes, when Gramps played with his Quirk too much—or when he ate too quickly or too messily—he got the hiccups. Hiccups caused all kinds of problems with Grandpa Quirk's magic. Problems they really didn't need while they were at school.

After a long moment, Molly turned her head and peeked at Penelope. "Do you have any ideas?" she asked.

Pen shook her head and her ponytail bounced back and forth.

"Should we talk it out together?" Molly asked.

Pen looked at her hopefully. "It can't hurt. You always get my mind going in the right direction—maybe if you tell me what you're thinking, it will spark some ideas or something."

"Okay," Molly agreed. "So I think the 'blume' hint must be important. Gramps told us to 'use what we read.' The clue says to 'follow the blume.'" She spoke slowly, just like Grandpa Quill had a moment ago when he'd repeated the hint. "Use what we *read*."

155

Penelope sat up straighter. "Oh!" She jumped up off the bench. "That's it."

"What's it?" Molly asked.

"You're a genius, Molly," Pen said. Molly looked at her like she was crazy—she was no closer to figuring out their grandpa Quill's final hiding place, but Penelope suddenly seemed much more sure. Pen grabbed Molly's hand and pulled her up. She said, "He was giving us another clue! He told us to 'use what you read.' Blume!"

In Penelope's mind, everything had snapped into place. But Molly was still one step behind. "Yes . . . I got all that, but I still don't get it," she said.

"*Judy* Blume!" Pen shouted. "Mom read us the book *Tales of a Fourth Grade Nothing* on our way to Normal this summer. It was written by Judy Blume!"

"Fudgie," Finn said, giggling. "I love Fudgie."

"Yes, Finn, the story with Fudge and Peter and the turtle." Pen grinned.

"And Turtle the dog!" Finn cheered. "Remember how they got that dog at the end because Fudge—"

Penelope cut him off. "Yep. So either this clue has something to do with turtles, or dogs, or naughty little boys . . . or the clue is hidden near her books! In the library!"

As Grandpa Quill cheered, Molly wrapped her sister into a snug hug. "Let's go find it!"

They ran toward the library. Grandpa Quill and Finn hustled along behind them. "You're getting warm," Grandpa Quill called out as they passed room six. "Warmer," he cried as they approached the door of the media center.

Mrs. Owens, the media teacher, waved to them as they came in. "You're here early today, girls. Something I can help you with? We just got a new shipment of Newbery winners in, if you'd like me to give you some suggestions."

"Not today, Mrs. Owens," Penelope said. "We're on the hunt for Judy Blume."

"Ah, yes," Mrs. Owens said. "Classic stories with a lot of humor. Some of my own kids' personal favorites."

157

Grandpa woo-hooed as the girls jogged over to the chapter book section. "Hot! You're burning up!"

Molly scanned the shelves and searched for "Blume, Judy."

"Here she is," she told Penelope. "She's written a million books."

Pen crouched down on the floor beside Molly, and they pulled out all of the Judy Blume books. Molly lay down on the floor and peeked into the empty hole on the shelf. She reached her hand back into the open space and felt around for their last gift.

Meanwhile, Pen paged through each of the books. "I found something!" She flipped open a paperback copy of *Superfudge* and found a green piece of paper tucked inside like a bookmark. One side of the paper was printed with cartoonish wiener dogs, and the other had handwritten words on it.

"Our last clue!" Molly said gleefully. "We did it, Pen!"

They gave each other a high five. Grandpa clapped from his seat in one of the cushy chairs by the window. Finn wiggled his way in between his sisters and said, "Hey, I was part of the team, too. Don't forget about me."

"You were an excellent assistant, Finn," Molly agreed. "Let's read it!"

Pen cleared her throat. "Here goes . . ."

Your final mini gift reveals too much,
And so you'll have to wait.
But tomorrow brings the mega gift,
And that you will not hate.
Where to look? That's up to you.
Just follow the sounds,
before you're too late . . .

Molly and Pen both glanced at their grandpa Quill, who had relaxed back into the smooshy library chair with his eyes closed. "No last mini gift, Gramps?" Molly asked, startling him out of his slumber.

Grandpa Quill opened one eye. "Not yet, I'm afraid. Just that final clue. I do *have* another mini gift, but if I gave it to you now, you'd be sure to put two and two and two together to figure out this year's theme. I don't want to reveal too much, so I'll give it to you tomorrow. *If* you're able to find your final gift in time, that is."

Molly put her hand on her hip. "So there *is* a theme to the mini gifts this year?" She looked at her sister, who shrugged. "All the mini gifts have seemed a little random to us."

"Of course there's a theme!" Grandpa said with a huff. "I've just been very sly about it."

"Okay," Pen said, studying the clue again. "Well, it looks like we have to wait until tomorrow to find our final present, huh?"

"That you do," Gramps said, bubbling with excitement. "And you better get ready, girls. Because I definitely saved the best for last!"

CHAPTER 18
Nerdy Cow

The big day had finally arrived: Molly and Penelope's real, official birthday. The week-long Quirkalicious Birthday Hunt had been a big part of the celebration, of course, but today the girls were actually *ten*.

After they'd found their last clue the previous morning, the rest of Friday crawled by. School had felt endless, and the evening had dragged on even more. Though they were both busy working on final preparations for their portion of their big party on Saturday, it felt like the day would never end.

"It looks great in here!" Molly exclaimed, rushing downstairs in her pajamas on Saturday morning. It looked like a birthday party explosion in their living room—streamers were twisted and hung along the walls and entryways, balloons bounced merrily around the edge of the room, confetti was sprinkled everywhere, and there was a big "Happy Birthday" banner tacked up over the front door.

Bree turned and smiled. "Happy birthday, dear." She and Gramps had gotten up early to decorate the house before the girls awoke. "How did you sleep?"

Molly yawned and sat on the bottom stair. "Not great. I was up super-late thinking about the last present in our Quirkalicious Birthday Hunt."

"You are going to love it," Bree said. "Where's your sister?"

"Still sleeping," Molly said, stifling another yawn.

"Well, go back upstairs and wake her. In not too long, Gramps will be ready for you to start hunting for the final present. I want you both to eat breakfast before you begin searching."

Molly did as she was told and trudged back upstairs. Before she woke her sister, though, Molly sat for a moment on the girls' bedroom window seat. She listened to the sounds of Pen's early-morning tossing, scratched Niblet's fluffy head, and watched Gran and Grandpa Quirk struggling to hang her piñata high in a tree. Gramps had put a collar and a leash on the piñata, which made the crepe paper cow look oddly real. Gran was using the leash to lift the piñata into the air.

As she sat there, Molly thought about the week, and how strange it had felt to argue with her sister about everything—their party, the Quirkalicious Birthday Hunt, the pet they'd wished for as a gift. Their birthday week had been bittersweet, and Molly hoped the party would go well so their year would start on the right note.

"This week was weird," Molly whispered into Niblet's ear, as though he could somehow make it better. "Pen and I never fight. You know that, don't you?" Niblet nuzzled closer and sighed. Molly leaned her head on his and said, "I'm sorry we couldn't convince Mom and Gramps to get another pet for you to play with." Niblet's eyes drifted closed as Molly rubbed the soft spot under his arm.

"Morning, Molly." Penelope's sleepy voice startled Molly.

"Good morning. Happy birthday, sister."

"You, too." Pen sat on the edge of the bed with her legs dangling down to the floor. Her hair was wild and huge from sleep, and her eyes looked tired. "Are we gonna look for our last present together this morning?"

Molly nodded. "I think we should."

"Me, too," Pen said, standing up to stretch. There was a long pause, then she asked, "So . . . are you all ready for your half of our party later?"

"I think so," Molly said. "I have some cool games planned, and the piñata is full of candy. Do you want to hear what else we're going to do?" When Pen nodded, Molly continued. "So Stella's mom is letting me borrow their Wii and this dance game that sounds super-fun. It's going to be a dance party, sort of. Mom's letting me move the TV out to the deck, just for the day."

165

"Oh," Pen said, yawning. "I'm sure everyone will love that."

"Can you tell me what you're doing for your part of the party, or is it still a secret?" Molly asked.

Penelope squeezed in beside Molly on the window seat and rubbed Niblet's other armpit. "Well, I was talking to Gran about some of my ideas. She found out that Mrs. DeVille has this old projector thingy that will show movies on our fence. She offered to let me use it for the party, so I'm going to put *The Wizard of Oz* on and everyone gets to make their own flavored popcorn balls. Nothing major."

"Wow," Molly said. She was a little jealous. Penelope was turning their yard into a movie theater, which was way cooler than a dance party on the deck. "That sounds great."

Pen glanced into the side yard and giggled when she saw Gran and Gramps wrestling with the piñata. "Do you think you should go down and help them? Your piñata seems to be causing some problems."

The girls hustled downstairs. They both stopped to give their mom a hug, then went out to the back deck with mugs full of cereal.

"Need some help?" Molly yelled to Gran and Grandpa Quill.

"Nope," Grandpa Quill said. "We're getting our system all worked out now. This cow will be mooing from her perch in no time."

Though Molly could see—very plainly—why they were having trouble lifting the piñata into the air, she said nothing. It was funny watching as Gran fluttered up, holding one end of the piñata-hanging rope. She tossed it over a thick tree branch, then dropped the loose end of rope down to Grandpa Quill on the other side. "This stinkin' cow just refuses to get up in that tree!" Grandpa Quill yowled, tugging at the end of the rope. Gran pulled up on the loop on the cow's leash. "It's too heavy for me to pull. The thing won't budge. There must be too much candy in your piñata, Molly."

Molly giggled. She was the only one who could see that invisible Finn was sitting atop the piñata. With the added weight of a five-year-old rider, Grandpa and Gran Quirk were *never* going to be able to hoist her cow piñata into the air. "The piñata has a passenger, Gramps."

167

"Blast!" Grandpa Quill yelled. He rushed over to the piñata and grabbed for Finn. But he was too slow. Finn slipped off the paper saddle and dashed away.

"Nah nah nah nah nah, you can't catch me!" Finn teased.

Grandpa Quill slumped back toward the piñata, and said, "Shall we give it another go, love? Without the boy?"

Gran whistled as she dragged the rope up and over the tree branch again. But before she could drop it into Grandpa's waiting arms, the piñata shifted over a few inches . . . and mooed.

"Whoa," Pen said, her eyes growing wide. Both she and Molly leaned down to set their cereal mugs on the deck. Just as the rope came tumbling down, the cow piñata turned in a slow, lazy circle. Then it dashed across the yard, pulling the rope and its leash behind. Pen gasped. "It's trying to escape!"

169

"Oh, man," Molly said. She ran into the yard, chasing after her piñata. The purple-and-pink crepe paper cow dodged back and forth, desperately searching for an escape route. Wrapped chocolates, lollipops, and other sweets rattled around inside its boxy stomach. "Penelope! I know you hate piñatas, but this is *not* the way to get out of having one at our party. Stop it."

"I can't stop it!" Pen yelled back. She really did *not* like piñatas, and she couldn't convince herself otherwise. Now that her mind had figured out how to get rid of it, she was finding it impossible to control her thoughts. She knew that if the cow escaped, that would mean bye-bye piñata at the party.

"Giddy-up!" Invisible Finn called from the far side of the yard. He ran toward the piñata at full speed. The cow dashed off, startled by the loud noise. It mooed at Molly when she got too close. Grandpa tried to corner it, but the cow kept shifting and galloping off into another area of the yard. They all backed off and watched as the frightened cow zigged and zagged around the grass.

Every time Molly went near, it looked up and snorted. After a few long, moo-filled minutes, the cow eventually settled into the back corner of the yard by the garage and chomped messily at a patch of grass. The leash dangled on the ground uselessly.

Grandpa Quill looked at the cow, then twirled his mustache. "I wonder . . . ," he said. "Hey, Finn. C'mere, kiddo." Finn strolled over and Gramps whispered something to him. They both giggled like toddlers and Finn slowly and quietly made his way toward the cow.

Molly watched from a few paces away as her invisible brother reached under the cow and grabbed for the crepe paper udders. Grandpa giggled again as Finn tugged gently at the underside of the cow, trying to milk it.

"Hey, look! It worked," Finn cried, holding out his tiny hand for Molly to see. "But Gramps, you were wrong. This moo doesn't have milk—it gives Nerds!"

CHAPTER 19

Follow the Sounds

Finn milked a cup full of sweets out of the cow before Pen's mind settled and the paper creature turned back into a normal candy-filled piñata again. Then Finn sat and ate his candy on the deck, giving Gran and Grandpa Quirk time to hang the piñata from the tree branch without any more distractions.

When they'd finished, Grandpa Quill strolled over to the deck and joined the kids. "Ladies," he said. "Finnegan." He grabbed a giant handful of sugary treats out of Finn's cup and popped them into his mouth. He mumbled through the candy, "Are you ready to start hunting for your super-de-duper final present, girls?"

Molly and Pen both leaped up. "Is it time?" Molly asked.

"I'm ready," Grandpa Quill said. "Are your ears open?"

Molly and Pen both craned their necks to see if they could hear anything. Their final clue had said: Where to look? That's up to you. Just follow the sounds, before you're too late . . ."

It wasn't much of a clue, and neither Molly nor Penelope really knew what to make of it. They'd both decided that looking near the stereo made sense, since that made plenty of sounds. Their brother made a ton of noise, the fridge was pretty loud, and the upstairs toilet made all kinds of funny clanking. But that was really as far as they'd gotten, since each girl had spent much of the previous night planning her half of their birthday party.

Pen was especially worried about the party going well—so she hadn't had as much time to focus on the last clue as she would have liked. She and Molly had each only invited a couple of people to their house—not a whole herd—which was helping Penelope remain somewhat calm about the afternoon. Stella, Norah, Amelia, and Izzy had been on both girls' invite lists. Penelope had also wanted to invite Joey, and Molly had invited a few other girls in their class. They'd reluctantly agreed to let Pierce Von Fuffenfluffer come, just to keep Finn happy and occupied. The party wouldn't start until late afternoon. That meant they could focus on birthday-present hunting until well after lunch.

"Is there anything else we need to know?" Molly asked Grandpa Quill as she grabbed the girls' cereal mugs off the deck. She shrugged and said, "Or do we just start listening for sounds to follow?"

Pen grumbled, "Such a helpful clue."

"I've gotta say, this clue will be easy to solve if you just listen," Grandpa Quill said. Molly was headed into the kitchen when he spoke up again. "Oh, and girls . . ."

"Yeah?" Pen asked.

"Your gran decided to have some fun with your final mini gift."

"I thought we didn't get a final mini gift?" Molly said. "Just the last clue."

"Actually," Pen blurted out, "the last clue said, 'Your final mini gift reveals too much, and so you'll have to wait.' Not that there *isn't* a final mini gift—Gramps did say we'd get it today." She smiled sweetly at their grandpa Quill. "Do we get our last mini gift now?"

He nodded, waved his hand through the air in a flourish, and said, "Wait no more, girls."

Molly and Pen both looked around and at the yard. Nothing happened.

Then, above them, their gran called, "Up here, girls." They turned their gaze upward, and watched as Gran slipped the

175

collar and leash off Molly's piñata. Holding the curled-up leash in her tiny arms, Gran flew over and placed them both in Penelope's hands.

"A collar?" Molly squeaked. "Is our last mini gift a collar and a *leash*?"

Grandpa smiled broadly. "Maybe . . ."

"It is!" Pen screamed. "Do you really mean it? If our final mini gift is a leash, does that mean our big present is—"

"A PET?" Molly and Pen yelled together.

"I hope it's a pig," Finn said. He rubbed his hands together and oinked, then popped a piece of gum into his mouth so they could all see the pig face he was making.

"Where is it, Gramps?" Pen asked.

Grandpa Quill shrugged. "My lips are sealed. This is *your* Quirkalicious Birthday Hunt, and I've helped you too much this week already. Go fetch your gift, girls."

Molly and Pen ran out into the yard and lis-tened carefully to see if they could hear anything. The yard was silent. Only the sound of birds and Finn's candy crunching. When they heard nothing else, they ran back to the deck. "I assume we're listening for something barking or meowing or oinking, right?" Pen asked.

Grandpa Quill said nothing, but Molly grinned. A pet! "Let's go inside," she suggested.

Gleefully, the girls ran into the house, slamming through the back door on their way to the living room. "Mom? Have you heard anything?" Pen asked.

Bree was sitting in her favorite chair in the living room with a cup of tea, surrounded by birthday party decorations. Mr. Intihar was sitting on the sofa, blowing up more balloons. The girls' mom had asked him to come over to help out with the party. Molly and Penelope both thought it was pretty cool that their teacher was coming to their birthday party. Even if he did act kind of weird around their mom.

When Bree realized the girls had started the search for their final present, she stood up to follow. Mr. Intihar's face was red from puffing up balloons, and he collapsed back on the couch to catch his breath. He took a deep gulp of air and called, "Morning, girls. Happy birthday to you on this, your most official birthday day!"

"Thanks, Mr. I.," Penelope said, blushing.

Molly echoed the thanks, then dashed to the living room window. Something was moving on the other side of the curtain. Mrs. DeVille, who barely ever left her house except for afternoon tea at the Quirks' house, was in the Quirks' front yard. She turned and saw Molly watching her through the window. When she realized she'd been spotted, Mrs. DeVille picked up her pace a bit and hustled out the gate, then across the lawn to her own front steps.

"What was Mrs. DeVille doing over here?" Molly wondered aloud.

Pen rushed to the window. "She was at our house?"

"In the yard," Molly said.

Pen's eyes grew wide. "Are you thinking what I'm thinking?"

Molly's face split into a ginormous grin. "Maybe she's in on it!"

Together, they yelled, "Let's check the yard!"

Both girls dashed for the front door. Finn and Grandpa Quill rushed through the back door just as the girls pulled the front door open. Mr. Intihar,

Bree, Grandpa Quill, and Finn crowded behind the twins as they made their way outside. Gran fluttered in the air nearby, hovering over a large, gift-wrapped box that was sitting in the side yard. When Gran saw Mr. Intihar, she zoomed behind a fluttering willow branch for cover.

The gift box was the size of a giant microwave and it had big, messy holes cut into it all over. "It has air holes!" Molly said with a gasp. "There's something living in there. It's making sounds!"

Penelope sucked in a breath and approached. "Whatever's in there is moving, too," she whispered. As the girls hustled toward the box, they heard faint whining sounds. Molly moved to one side of the box, and Penelope went to the other. "On three," Molly ordered. She and Pen both put their hands on the box and prepared to lift off the cover. Penelope's hands were shaking, and Molly's stomach was jittery and excited.

"One . . . ," Finn said quickly. Then he rushed to add, "Two, three!"

179

Molly and Pen tugged gently, jiggling the box top to try to loosen it. Whatever was inside began to whine a bit louder. The box top slid up, up, up.

"What do you think it is?" Molly asked, practically bubbling over with excitement. Just as they were about to whisk it open, a snorty sound exploded behind them.

Hiccup! Grandpa Quill covered his mouth as the whole family shot back in time.

CHAPTER 20

wHaT's Dat?

Hiccup!

"No!" Molly screamed as time flapped and flopped—back and forth.

Hiccup!

They zoomed five seconds backward, then two seconds forward. Only Molly and Grandpa Quill realized what was happening, but *everyone* was along for the ride.

"It was the piñata treats," Grandpa Quill told Molly, uselessly trying to cover his mouth to keep

181

the hiccups inside. "I don't do well with that much sugar before noon."

Hiccup!

The whole group was suddenly back inside the house. Pen was just about to pull open the front door. She shook her head, trying to clear away the fog that followed Grandpa Quill's hiccups.

Pen reached for the door again, and they all rushed out to the front porch. There was the box in the yard. Molly and Pen ran down the steps and reached for the lid, for the second time. Then:

Hiccup!

Now they were in the backyard. Once again, Gran was flying toward them with the leash and collar wrapped in her arms. Before any of them could move forward from there, Grandpa Quill hiccuped *again*.

Hiccup!

This time, he'd hiccuped them forward. The girls were slipping the lid of the box off. Mr. Intihar and Bree and Finn and Penelope all scratched their heads, blinking to try to figure out why they felt so woozy.

Molly waited for a moment as everyone got

their bearings. Then, just as she and Penelope were about to pull their gift box open that final inch, Molly glanced at Grandpa Quill. He was holding his breath to try to stop the hiccups for good.

"C'mon, Molly," Penelope urged. "Let's see what it is!"

Grandpa Quill nodded at Molly and said, "I'm good now. Carry on."

Mr. Intihar looked faint and confused after all the bopping back and forth through time. He crumpled in an exhausted heap on the porch swing, his eyes cloudy and distant. Grandpa Quill sat down on the other side of the swing and fought to keep his eyes open. Time-twisting made Grandpa extra snoozy.

Molly and Penelope gave the box top one last tug and leaned over to see what was inside.

"A puppy!" Molly gushed. "Oh my gosh, it's a puppy. You got us a *puppy*!"

Bree and Grandpa Quill both beamed. Penelope reached inside the box and pulled out the fluffiest, puffiest little ball of fur she'd ever seen. Though she'd longed for a cat, even Pen had to admit that the little creature in her arms was one of the cutest dogs on earth. She squinted and brought her face close to the puppy's snout. A soft pink tongue popped out of the little dog's mouth and licked Pen's nose.

Pen passed the puppy to her sister. Molly buried her face in the soft black-and-white spotted fur.

"What do you think?" Grandpa Quill asked.

"I love it!" Molly cooed. "He's perfect."

"She," Bree said. "It's a little girl. She's a mix of Pomeranian and poodle—they call it a Pomapoo—and she was just waiting for us at the shelter. She needed a loving home, and this little girl seemed like the right kind of pal for our snuggly Niblet." Bree quickly realized her mistake and glanced at Mr. Intihar with a worried frown on her face. But the girls' teacher was so dazed after Grandpa Quill's bout of hiccups that he hadn't heard a thing. Bree added, "Mrs. DeVille has been keeping her for us for a few days so you girls wouldn't find out. Did we keep a good secret?"

"Very good!" Molly exclaimed. "I had no idea." She got a far-off look in her eyes and said, "Do you think *this* is why Nibbly snuck over to Mrs.

DeVille's house? I bet he wanted to meet his new sister."

"Nibbly?" Mr. Intihar asked, shaking his head. "Whose sister?"

Bree patted his arm and said, "Just ignore us, George."

"Right," Mr. Intihar said with a sleepy nod. "Will do."

Penelope studied their new puppy as Molly cradled the ball of fluff in her arms. "You know, I thought I wanted a cat," Pen said thoughtfully. "But I have to admit . . . this little peanut actually *looks* an awful lot like a kitten with all that fuzzy hair. It's sort of the same, I guess, except she barks and whines

instead of purring. She's so furry and teensy and cute." Pen narrowed her eyes, trying to imagine what the puppy would look like with more feline features and a longer tail. "She actually looks a little bit like a dog-cat, doesn't she?"

Molly gasped as, suddenly, the little puppy's tail began to grow. Short, catlike whiskers popped out of the area next to the puppy's nose, and the dog's pupils took on a yellowish tinge. "Pen! Stop!"

"Oh, dear," Bree said, looking toward Mr. Intihar.

But Penelope's mind was racing now. The dog was adopting more catlike qualities with each passing second. Suddenly, the tiny dog released a strange, high-pitched *meow* and began to purr in Molly's arms.

"That's not fair!" Molly hissed, clutching the dog more tightly to her chest. "You cannot turn our dog into a cat."

"Oh dear, oh dear, oh dear," Bree said. She looked at Mr. Intihar and said, "You know, I could really go for some more coffee. You could, too, couldn't you, George? While you're in there, maybe you could grab a few squares of chocolate? I'm feeling a bit off."

Meanwhile, the little critter squirmed to escape from Molly's arms. When she finally climbed the front steps and let it down on the wooden porch, the puppy-with-a-cat-tail pranced across the wide wooden floorboards. It held its tail high, then leaped up onto the railing of the front porch. "It leaps like a cat!" Finn hollered.

Mr. Intihar sat up straight on the porch swing, blinked, and said, "Well, look at that little cutie." His jolting movements woke Grandpa Quill beside him. Mr. Intihar suddenly stood up and shook out his legs. "Huh. I think I fell asleep for a minute there. Coffee . . . I could use some coffee . . . And Bree, why don't I get you some chocolate." He just stood there, though, not fetching anything.

Grandpa Quill opened one eye and pulled a tennis ball out of his pocket. "Fetch, little lass," he said, then tossed the ball to the other side of the porch. The puppy wagged its kitten tail, and rushed over to the other side of the porch to play fetch. "Now do you girls understand the rest of your mini gifts?"

"The tennis ball I get," Pen said. "For playing fetch."

"The brush makes sense. And the bowl must be for the dog," Molly added. "That's why you laughed when I was eating my cereal out of it."

"What about the letter stickers?" Molly asked.

"You can decorate her dog dish with her name," Bree said. "It will be a one-of-a-kind dish, made with love."

"Oh, that will be fun. What's with the piece of gold? Our first mini gift?" Pen asked.

"When you figure out the perfect name for her, we can have it engraved and affix that nameplate to her collar," Grandpa Quill explained.

"She does need a name," Molly said as she and Penelope watched the dog-cat critter carefully. Though it had the body of a small puppy, it now had that distinctly catlike tail. Its mouth and nose were all pup, but the whiskers and eyes were one hundred percent cat. "For our very original dog that leaps like a cat."

"But fetches like a dog," Pen noted.

"She purrs," Molly continued.

The dog let out a little yip to let them know it

would really like to continue the game of fetch. "But our puppy also barks," Pen added.

Finn picked up the tennis ball and tossed it to the puppy. "It's not a dog anymore. It's a dat!"

"A dat?" Pen asked.

Mr. Intihar shook his head and ran his hand through his mess of hair. "A dat? A *who's* that?"

"Pen turned it into a *dat*," Finn said. "A dog that kinda looks and acts like a cat."

"Pen did what now?" Mr. Intihar asked. He stretched his arms over his head and moved toward the front door.

"Coffee, George. All you're thinking about is coffee." Bree fixed her eyes on Mr. Intihar's and smiled brightly.

Mr. Intihar nodded. "Yes. You know, I think I need a bit more coffee. Bree, do you mind if I help myself to another cup in the kitchen?"

"Not at all," Bree said. She hid a smile behind her hand.

Once Mr. Intihar had left, the Quirk kids got down on their knees on the front porch and surrounded their new pet. "Should we take her up to meet Niblet? Officially, this time?" Pen wondered.

"He's going to be so excited she's here to stay," Molly exclaimed.

The dog-cat critter continued to purr and yip and leap and lunge. Finn pulled it onto his lap and said, "What's your name, dude? Can you sit, little dat?"

"Aw, pickles," Grandpa Quill said, shaking his head. "I forgot to get puppy treats for training."

Pen and Molly looked at each other, then began to laugh. "Gramps, that's perfect," Molly said.

Grandpa Quill looked confused.

Penelope grinned and said, "Pickles. Let's call her Pickles. Hi, Pickles." She reached behind the critter's ears and scratched. Pickles flipped onto her back for a belly rub and purred while she wagged her tail madly.

"We have a dog that acts like a cat," Molly said quietly. "A dat. That's a pet that fits our family absolutely perfectly."

"A dat," Pen said thoughtfully. "I like it. I hope she stays this way."

"Me, too. You know what?" Molly began. "It's kinda like we both got what we were wishing for."

"It's a Molly-Pen combo," Pen agreed. "Which is

way cooler than just a plain old dog or a regular old cat, don't you think?"

Molly grinned as Pickles climbed into her lap. "We make a good team," Molly said. Then she realized that was true with everything. She and her sister were better clue hunters together, they had better ideas together, and they just *clicked* together. They wouldn't always agree on everything, but they made a really good duo. Molly scooted over so her sister could have a piece of Pickles on her lap, too. "Do you think maybe we should blend our ideas for our party? If we could figure out a way to smush all our ideas into one big plan, it would probably be a lot more fun and interesting than having our parties separately, don't you think?"

Pen nodded as Pickles purred and wagged, nuzzled and yipped. "I do. In fact, I am very sure this is going to be the best birthday party *ever.*"

CHAPTER 21

A Quirky Party

All of Molly's and Pen's friends arrived a few hours later, ready to party. Seven friends from school were dropped off, and Grandpa Quill quickly jumped into full entertaining mode. He was sharing all his worst jokes, and telling stories to entertain anyone who would listen. But he kept dozing off before he finished any of them. Finn had run off with his friend Pierce, and (with the exception of a few badly designed booby traps) they were staying mostly out of the way.

Pickles was snuggling upstairs with Niblet,

193

who'd quickly adopted the fluffy *dat* as a perfect little sister. The two had hit it off immediately. Niblet was happy to take care of her—and share some of his favorite sock chew toys—in the twins' room while the party was in full swing. Molly had promised to bring Niblet a piece of cake later if he promised to behave and stay out of view while taking good care of their new family pet.

Before their friends showed up, Molly and Penelope had worked together to build a superstar, super-tall cake that made a perfect centerpiece for their birthday party. The chocolate cake Martha had baked for Molly was used as a sturdy, scrumptious base. Then all of Penelope's frilly, flowery cupcakes were stacked carefully on top like a sugary pyramid. Gran had picked a beautiful, miniature fall bouquet that they perched up on the very top of the cake. Now they had a chocolate-vanilla cake tower that looked amazing and was sure to taste delicious.

Mr. Intihar and Martha had set out all the other food—grilled cheese, strawberries, sweet potato fries, and Martha's famous noodle kugel—while Bree poured the kids' drinks. Everyone

dished up plates and hustled out to the yard to eat in front of the giant movie screen. Mr. Intihar and Martha and Bree all sat in chairs on the back deck and kept an eye on the party from a distance. Molly could hear them laughing, and she celebrated the fact that their mom had begun to find such great friends in Normal.

The Wizard of Oz played on the big screen in the backyard while everyone milled around and played the yard games Gran and Gramps had set up that afternoon. Though she'd initially spied on the party through the hole in the fence, Mrs. DeVille eventually hobbled over to get a plate of Martha's kugel. She kept her distance from all the kids, muttering quiet comments to Gran over in the shadowy side yard, but Molly was sure she was having a good time.

When the movie ended, they set up Molly's dance game on the giant movie screen. All the partygoers took turns dancing and laughing, while everyone else looked on (including Niblet and Pickles, who were spying on the party from an upstairs window). The girls had found a way to do

just about everything both of them
the party was turning out absolutel'

"Time for the piñata!" Bree cal
the kids over.

Penelope cringed, while everyone else cheered.
Pen still hated the idea of piñatas. She didn't like
that they were all supposed to whap at the poor
cow with a big stick. Even still, she'd agreed to the
piñata since Molly really wanted one. What Pen
didn't know, though, was that Molly had worked
out a plan with Gran to keep the crepe paper cow
safe from harm.

"I wanna go first!" Finn cried, running out to the
backyard. He swung a stick around in the air, nearly
whacking his friend Pierce on the head. Pierce
ducked, then chased after Finn to get in line.

While all the kids lined up, Gran Quirk hid high
in the tree. She'd borrowed Pickles's leash and collar and attached it to the cow again. At Molly's
request, Gran tugged the piñata up every time
someone swung at it. So no one was able to hit it!

"This must be some kind of trick piñata," Joey
muttered, after he'd swung and missed three times.

"I think we all just have really bad aim," Norah explained patiently. "It's not like the piñata can run away from us. Blame yourself, not the cow."

"I play baseball!" Joey growled. "There's no way I could miss so many times. My swing is outta this world."

Izzy rolled her eyes. "Not today, it isn't."

Eventually, when it was clear no one was going to land a hit, Bree tugged at the cow's crepe paper udders, which opened up the flap on the bottom of the piñata's belly. Candy rained down on everyone, and the cow swung from its perch—still intact.

Finn picked up a bunch of chocolate kisses and started throwing them at everyone. When Molly wasn't looking, he slipped his gum out of his mouth and hid in a corner of the yard. Every time someone came near, he pelted them with a chocolate kiss.

"Hey!" Amelia yelped, as a chocolate bounced off her arm.

"Yow!" Stella screeched, searching for the source of the chocolate attack. Finn giggled and squirmed backward into the high grass against the fence. Luckily, Grandpa Quill's crazy dancing in front of the giant movie screen quickly distracted everyone.

He and Mr. Intihar were dancing up a storm as they tried to follow the moves on the screen. All the kids at the party laughed watching them, then everyone joined in as the song came to a close.

"You know what I think?" Molly asked, wrapping her arm around her twin sister as they danced alongside their friends. "I think we planned the *perfect* party."

Bree walked out onto the deck with the towering chocolate-and-vanilla cake teetering in her arms. In the waning light of the early evening, everyone at the party began to sing "Happy Birthday."

"I think you're right," Pen said, smiling happily. "This was the best birthday ever. I wouldn't want to share a birthday with anyone other than you, Quirkalicious sister."

As all their friends crowded around, Molly and Pen both felt a rush of happiness. Together, they leaned forward and—*whoosh!*—blew out all the candles on their cake. Though neither girl said her wish out loud, they had both wished for the same thing: that the year ahead of them in Normal, Michigan, would be the Quirks' best year ever!